Short Stories

For the Weird Kids

By J. L. Wolf

Dedicated to the weirdos

# Introduction

I have a bit of a soft spot for anything strange and creepy. Urban legends, ghost stories and haunted places are things that I'm just naturally drawn to, which apparently isn't odd for a Capricorn so let's put it down to that. When I was young I would stay up late on my dad's old computer for as long as I could keep my eyes open, scrolling through Google for all the ghost stories I could find. Before I knew it, hours had passed and my mind was full of malevolent and misunderstood spirits, killer clowns, possessed babysitters and all the other creepy things I had read, which would probably explain a lot of the weird dreams I had as a child.

My favourite book growing up was called 'The Phantom Fisherboy' and was a collection of old Victorian ghost stories. I still have it, and I've read it so many times the pages are falling out and the front cover has disappeared completely. I think I lost it down the side of a bed or something back in 1999.

My first best friend and I bonded over stories. Every morning whilst we were walking into school together she would ask me to tell her what I had gotten up to the night before. She wasn't actually inquiring about my evening habits, but that question was in fact my que to ramble off a strange tale that I had been thinking of since I'd first woken up that morning and I would proceed to tell her how portals had opened in my bedroom walls or a tiny goblin had leapt up onto my bed, granting me three wishes in exchange for my brother...

I was, what most would refer to as; a 'weird kid'. I valued time alone over playing with friends, I liked the dark and things that would scare most others, and above all – I was fascinated with the 'other side'. As you've probably guessed I wasn't that popular, but I didn't really want to be. So that worked out just fine.

At around 12 years old, I started writing down all the short stories that came to my head. Not really for any particular purpose; I just enjoyed writing them and reading them out to my sisters to freak them out before bed. My room was full of old notebooks and scraps of paper covered in writing and half-finished stories, which is pretty much how my office is now. I'm a writer – not an organizer.

The question I get asked most often from people who read my work is; "Do you actually believe that the things you write about exist?"

When they say 'things I write about', what they mean is ghosts, aliens, vampires and mermaids etc. My answer is always the same; of course. Asking if I believe in such things is like asking if I believe in, to quote Terry Pratchett; the postman. Not only do I believe in them, but I'm sure if you do enough Googling on your dad's old computer – you will do.

# Contents

| | |
|---|---|
| Ula | 6 |
| Grandma's Secret | 29 |
| Ouija | 34 |
| Denny | 41 |
| Mermaids | 46 |
| The Devils Mask | 51 |
| The Thing in my Daughter's Bedroom | 54 |
| Boy in the Window | 57 |
| The Vampires Child | 64 |
| Operation Stargate | 70 |
| Stairs in the Woods | 77 |
| The Vampire of Highgate | 82 |
| Project Black Box | 89 |
| Mama Llarona | 99 |
| Bunny Man Bridge | 106 |
| Google Earth | 112 |
| The Ticking in the Walls | 115 |
| The Lady at 305 | 125 |
| Slenderman | 133 |
| Viral | 143 |
| Guy | 152 |
| The Children of Wolfpit | 159 |
| The Worlds Below | 165 |
| Abduction | 169 |
| An Interview with the Devil | 175 |
| Woman in White | 179 |

# Ula

## Introduction

Scientists think that nearly all porpoises and dolphins descended from carnivorous land animals called Mesonychids that were part of the fauna 60 million years ago. Mesonychids were similar to wolves that took to the waters in search for food. They developed fins, adapted their teeth to better suit marine life and shed all of their hair, becoming the sea creatures we know today in a remarkable evolutionary process.

150,000 years ago a group of brown bears separated from the rest of their species and just like the Mesonychids they took to the waters in search of food. Over time they developed webbing between their paws, learnt to hold their breath, and even changed colour. This group of brown bears became the polar bears we know today and their evolution is still happening right in front of us.

6.5 billion years ago, off the coast of East Africa, both food and land were becoming sparse for our early ancestors due to overpopulation and inhospitable conditions.

Small groups of early humans would collect along the shoreline to hunt for fish, learning to move in the waters, swim and hold their breath for minutes at a time. These groups became more adapted to the water and eventually, they moved their homes into the rock pools and caves that surrounded the sea, developing their intelligence with the iodine and fatty acids in the shellfish they ate. They began to shed their hair, developed webbing between their fingers and toes, evolving more and more to suit life in the water. As the humans changed, so did the land. East Africa was exploding with volcanoes and earthquakes, forcing a large portion of the population further inland and underground, but another group found a different escape, one they were already adapting to.

This is their story, the sea people's story.

# Chapter One

My name is Dr Mason Walsh and I'm a marine biologist. For the past 21 years I've been working alongside an organization called NOAA, which stands for the National Oceanic and Atmospheric Administration. Our main focus is collecting information on the conditions of the oceans, atmosphere and ecosystems as well as protecting threatened or endangered marine species, like whales.

On the 27th of August 2004 the US Navy began testing some new sonar weaponry which involved emitting harmful low frequency waves. On the 28th of August 2004, 72 whales, 26 dolphins and one unidentified creature where found beached along the Washington state. Only one piece of footage was ever taken of the unidentified creature before it was taken away and that was confiscated by the US Navy shortly afterwards.

My team and I arrived on the scene about 8:20am. We noticed what looked like a hundred whales and a few dolphins up and down the beach; they all had blood coming out of their ears. It was important for us to collect blood and tissue samples to determine the cause of death – which at this point didn't appear to be suffocation – the usual case with beaching. As we headed down to the first group of whales I noticed a small section of the beach cornered off. Men in Hazmat suits appeared to be working on something, almost like they were giving it medical attention while government officials questioned them behind a small white tent. I remember thinking that was weird, in all the years we've been collecting samples from these types of events I'd never seen men in Hazmat suits with white tents up. Within the hour they had gone and taken with them whatever they were studying in a black van, they hadn't even touched the whales. We didn't talk about it at the time; I guess we were just trying to get the job done.

We took our samples back to the lab. I noticed what looked like white circles in the cells, which is common in cases where blunt force trauma is the cause of death but not suffocation. We knew it was the sonar weaponry testing that had caused of death of all these animals somehow, whatever they were testing had caused significant harm to marine life and if we were going to do anything to protect these animals and stop this kind of underwater testing in the future we needed proof. We have underwater microphones all around the area, one that just so happened to be close by, so we pulled it up.

When you study dolphin and whale calls, after some time you start to see their language emerging. Certain calls are greetings or flirtatious gestures; others are calls for distress or hunger. Each call has a meaning – like our words. We'd been coding their language for some time now and had an idea of what pretty much each call meant. After we pulled up the microphone and played it back, we couldn't believe what we were hearing.

It started out normal, noisy, you could hear the usual chatter of dolphins and whales – it was clear there were a lot of them in the area, but after a few minutes it went completely silent. After a moment we heard this deep sonic boom that went on for quite some time, which was obviously the sonar testing that was being done by the Navy.

And then it happened.

The cries were haunting. There were literally hundreds of Whales and dolphins all using distress calls, all screaming in pain at the same time. I was in shock, just hearing it was awful. The recording went on for about fifteen minutes and you could tell it was torturous for them. I was more determined than ever to document what I had found and get justice. I sat there for hours listening to it, documenting all the different identifiable animals and the calls, times, events... I was so focused on taking down the Navy I almost missed it.

In the middle of the cries of the whales and the dolphins was a call I'd never heard before. It was much more intricate, almost like a complex, intelligent language.

I isolated the call and listened to it over and over again. I slowed it down to a third of the speed, to what we would be able to hear normally – it was enchanting, like nothing I'd ever heard before. I must have played it a thousand times that night; I didn't leave my office until 3am. I called in some of my team members and we compared it to a bloop signature from 1997. A bloop signature is basically a call from an unidentified creature. They seemed to be of the same species.

At the time I thought we may have uncovered some kind of new species of dolphin. I took the findings to the head of audio research at Cape Town University, and from there we uncovered something I don't think any of us could have imagined.

[Dr Mason Walsh, Marine Journal 2012]


My name is Selig Huldiberaht. I'm a German fisherman from Rugen, an island on the Baltic Sea. My father was a fisherman too, so I spent most of my life on the sea, learning to sail and fish when I was only a boy. I've known about the spears since I can remember, I think everyone around here knows about them.

The spears range in size, they're mostly small – the size of your forearm or smaller, but I've seen some the size of a man before. They're made using wood or bone and stingray barbs or broken glass and we find them a lot in fish, as if the fish was already being hunted before we caught it. They'd been washing up along the shores since my father could remember and for a long time people used to collect them, but after a while they lost interest, like most things.

It was June or July, sometime around then in 1994. I was out on my boat with a few crew members, it was early morning, and we were bringing in the first catch of the day. As we were pulling the net up, we saw something pulling itself out of it. One of my crew members had a camera on him, he liked taking pictures of the whales – so he took a few photos as it jumped back into the water and swam away.

When we pulled the net in we noticed one of the fish had a spear stuck in its side and a wound just below it as if it had been speared a second time.

After we got the pictures developed we saw what looked like a man or a woman in the water, only their bottom half looked like a tail. The picture was too fuzzy to be absolutely sure but for everyone who saw it, that is just what it was.

We never saw it again, but I know sightings like this are not uncommon for people who spend a lot of time on the sea.

[Selig Huldiberaht, BBC News 2008]


I'm Karmen Osbourne. I live in Seattle and I'm a professor in marine ecology and a research assistant at NOAA. My favourite colour is orange and my favourite animal is a dolphin, but if mermaids exist then I chose them. Sorry dolphins.

A year before the beaching in Washington State there where two more incidents, one in South Africa and one in Japan, both of these happened under similar circumstances involving Navy sonar weapons testing, and within only days of each other.

I'd travelled to Cape Town with Dr Mason Walsh and a few other members of our team to view samples and data for research of these events. During this time we were working closely with the audio research team at Cape Town University, we looked at their findings of the whale calls just before the hit and noticed that amongst the whale cries, another call could be heard – just like what happened in Washington. We sent the call off to other research facilities around the world and waited to hear back from someone, it was 18 days before we got a response. I'll never forget what it said, or what happened in the weeks after.

[Karmen Osbourne, The deep sea diaries, 2011]


My name is Eiichi Okamoto. I'm a deep sea diver from Japan and was present during the whale beaching of 2003.

I've been diving for the last 15 years and have swam with almost every undersea creature there is, including hammerhead sharks and orcas.

The day before the beaching there was a number of dolphins in the area, we tell our children when you see lots of dolphins, it's because the mermaids have come out to play. We believe in mermaids in Japan and sightings are not uncommon. On the day of the beaching, rumours went around of a woman, a woman with a fish tail sat on the rocks far out to sea, crying at the sight of the beached whales and dolphins. According to the people, she was seen jumping in and out of the water, staying under for up to fifteen minutes at a time.

When I was there I didn't see a woman with a fish tail on the rocks – then again, I wasn't looking at the rocks, I was looking at the whales. What I did see however, was someone swimming, which I thought was weird considering what was going on. They dived when they saw me looking and I didn't see them again. I can't say what or who it was for sure, I only saw a head - it was just odd.

[Eiichi Okamoto, Diver Blogs, 2006]

# Chapter Two

My name is [withheld] I actually started off as a solutions architect in IT security with the US navy. I was based in Washington DC for four years before being relocated to [Location withheld.] When I first came here I didn't know what to expect, my work had always been in IT security and so I expected to be developing some sort of software, I just didn't know what for.

I was told it would some kind of firewall to protect top secret information from hackers but didn't have anything else to go on until I actually entered the lab. I don't think words could quite so eloquently describe how I felt when I first saw her. They'd named her Ula, which means Jewel of the sea, and by God was she a jewel. She wasn't scaled like a fish like I thought she would be, but her skin shone in the light like some kind of crystal. She didn't speak either, she used a form of songlike whale call and gestures and body language to communicate.

My office wasn't in the lab, but I was allowed in at certain times to observe her. I put my hand up to the glass once hoping she'd come and see me, placing her hand on top of mine like we were long lost lovers and giving me the moment of a life time. She didn't. She stayed behind the rocks, hiding from us all. Even when she was being more sociable she would never come that close to us, or make eye contact for very long, the only one she really interacted with was her handler; Lucy, and apparently that was a relationship that took years to build.

She doesn't trust us, Ula. She calls us 'the different ones' or 'the changed ones', only referring to us as the 'dark haired land person' or 'the fat land person' etc. She's rather blunt and insensitive when it comes to people. The only time she really shows emotion is when she talks of the dolphins, whales or her family back in the ocean.

It wasn't until 2009 she mastered sign language and they began their interrogations. Most of us felt sorry for her, she always looked terrified and uncomfortable as they pressed her with invasive questions. If she refused to answer them, they would refuse to feed her or would keep her out of the water until she was close to death.

[March 4th 2009, extract from Journal, name withheld.]

Ice-wall security software updated, enhancements awaiting instalment; scheduled for 23:00 hours.

Ula making progress, has full understanding of sign language and is now using it to communicate with her handler and a select few researchers on almost a daily basis. Rarely showing signs of distress or depression, has adapted well to her surroundings.

[March 5th 2009, extract from journal, name withheld.]

Ice-wall enhancements at 72% completion, 07:00 hours.

Ula using distress calls today, not signing at all with handler and refused food until researchers were leaving lab. Signed 'homesick' to handler just before she left, researchers arranging for Lucy and other divers to enter tank and attempt at socializing with her, hopefully taking place on 7th, requesting access to observation deck.

[March 6th 2009, extract from journal, name withheld]

Ice-wall enhancements stalled, error message: 2510B809. Installing back up programme.

Back up programme installed.

Two divers fluent in sign language due to enter tank at 08:00 tomorrow. Second entry will be at 13:00. Team will meet in lab at 06:00 for briefing. Request to viewing deck accepted.

[March 7th 2009, extract from journal, name withheld.]

Back up programme working sufficiently. Ice-wall scheduled for beta test.

Heading to observation deck.

06:00. Team briefing took place in lab in front of tank. Ula's handler stood at tank walls and translated to Ula in sign language what would be happening. She seemed frightened at first, but relaxed after a while and trusted they had no intentions to harm her. Team was given distress signals and will be equipped with head cameras to record encounter.

07:00. Equipment testing.

08:00. The dive.

Lucy was the first diver to enter the water. Once we got to the viewing deck the divers and a few other SEALS opened the cage at the top of the tank. The divers entered the water one by one, Lucy first, [name withheld] second, and [name withheld] third. They spaced each dive out with a few minutes between so as not to overwhelm Ula.

08:15, entry successful, Ula curious about equipment and interacting playfully with divers, mostly Lucy, signing to come with her and showing them around the tank.

09:00, Ula seems to be favouring Lucy over the other two divers, which was expected – but she seems to be actively dragging Lucy away from them and deeper into the tank. Lucy has not put out a distress signal and so no intervention is taking place.

10:00, the divers exit the tank, some concern is being shown over the way Ula took to Lucy and head of research is wondering if any harm was intended. Lucy protests Ula's innocence and says she was just over excited. The next dive will go ahead as scheduled.

11:00, Ula is swimming closer to the glass walls of her tank than recorded previously, looking out into the lab and watching us. Every now and again Lucy will go up to the tank and they will converse before Ula swims off.

13:00, second dive. This time Lucy is the last into the tank, the researchers want to know how Ula will respond to divers she barely knows. She doesn't respond well. Once she realises neither of the divers is Lucy she swims to the bottom of her tank and does not return until Lucy is in the water, after that she seems much more comfortable interacting with the other two divers. It seems overall she is still extremely anxious around us.

14:00, Ula has been interacting with all three divers successfully and displaying peaceful and playful behaviours. The divers exit the tank, Lucy is the last to leave, her and Ula touch hands before separating. It is clear from the dive Ula is a curious, intelligent and peaceful creature.

[March 8th 2009, extract from journal, name withheld.]

06:00, commencing updates to ice-wall.

Updates completed.

Software installation scheduled for 23:00 hours.

I go to see Ula before I pack up for the night. She's using distress calls again, I don't see Lucy anywhere. I try to comfort her at the side of the tank but it's not me she wants, she hides in the rocks. I give up and leave, not wanting to frighten this marvellous creature.

[March 10th 2009, extract from journal, name withheld.]

The video footage from dive as well as a transcript of all communications has finally been released for those on the observation deck. The video is wonderful, so detailed. I have a copy of Ula's signed conversation with the divers here:

Ula: "Lucy."

Lucy: "Hello Ula."

Ula: "Who are these land people?"

Lucy: "These are my friends, [name withheld] and [name withheld]"

Diver 1: "Hello Ula."

Ula: "Hello."

Diver 2: "Hello Ula. You are very beautiful."

Ula: "Thank you."

Lucy: "They want to meet you and speak with you."

Ula: "Why?"

Lucy: "You are very interesting; they want to learn more about your people and what we can do to protect you."

Ula: "The land people do not protect, they harm and kill, even each other."

Diver 1: "We know you don't trust us, please let us prove to you we're not all like that."

Ula: "You have me in prison."

Diver 2: "We're sorry for the circumstances, we wish it could be another way but we've never met anyone like you before, we didn't know what to do, we still don't."

Ula: "I am not happy."

Lucy: "What will make you happy?"

Ula: "Home."

Lucy: "One day, one step at a time. For now shall we just talk?"

Ula: "I don't want to talk. I want to swim."

Diver 2: "We can swim with you, would you like to show us around?"

Ula: "Ok. Follow."


Ula: "I miss my friends."

Lucy: "I know, I'd love to meet them one day."

Ula: "They wouldn't come near you, they would be afraid."

Lucy: "You could tell them about me, let them know I wouldn't hurt them."

Ula: "They would think I had gone insane."

Diver 1: "So your people have never interacted with land people before?"

Ula: "Never, we have stories of our ancient ancestors who sometimes visited the lands, one of our mothers fell in love with a land person once and tried to cut her tail down the middle so she could have legs and join him. The blood attracted sharks and she was eaten."

Diver 2: "I think we have a version of that story, but in ours she gets legs by magic and moves to the land to be with him."

Ula: "Land people are destructive, selfish and greedy, even you."


Lucy: "Are you upset with me?"

Ula: "No. You are my only friend here."

Lucy: "Where are you going?"

Ula: "Come with me."

Lucy: "What can we do to make you trust us?"

Ula: "Nothing. We are too different."

Lucy: "We're not that different."

Ula: "I would never do this to you."

Diver 1: "Hey Ula, what's this?"
Ula: "My spear."
Diver 1: "You hunt in here?"
Ula: "No, I just enjoy making them."
Diver 2: "Do you like to hunt, Ula?"
Ula: "Yes."

Diver 2: "Do you eat the fish in here?"
Ula: "No. They drop fish in for me to eat."
Diver 1: "So are these ones just for company?"
Ula: "Yes."

Lucy: "We could get you some more things for in here if you like, a shipwreck to explore? What do you think?"
Ula: "I've explored a lot of shipwrecks."
Diver 1: "We could get you a submarine wreckage, or an aeroplane?"
Ula: "I don't want anything."

Diver 2: "What is it like living in the ocean?"
Ula: "Peaceful. Until the US navy kidnap you."

Lucy: "Let her get used to you."

Ula: "Follow."
Lucy: "Where are we going?"
Ula: "This is where I sleep."

Diver 1: "Is there anything specific we can do to aid the protection of your people?"

Ula: "Yes. Leave us alone."

Diver 1: "Perhaps there are specific areas you keep too that we can put under our protection?"

Ula: "You just want to know where you can find us."

Lucy: "Ula, please, they want to help you."

Ula: "Land people only help themselves."


Ula: "You are leaving now?"

Lucy: "Yes."

Ula: "Will you come back?"

Lucy: "Of course I will, I'm here with you every day."


End of transcript.

They haven't released one from the second dive yet.

## Chapter Three

I took the findings to the head of audio research at Cape Town University, and from there we uncovered something I don't think any of us could have imagined.

When we got to Cape Town we'd actually planned on stopping off at the hotel for lunch before heading down to the University, but we got a message urging us to get there straight away and so we did.

We arrived at 16:00 and were greeted at the entrance by the head of audio research; Dr Mike Pittah. He took us down to the lab were they had a number of findings for us to examine, the first one was a recording taken during the time of the Navy testing. It was similar to the recording we had taken, the usual chatter and noise of marine life, a moment of silence, and then the deep sonic boom. I prepared myself for the wailing and crying of the animals, my heart thudding in my chest and my throat dry. It was much louder than Washington State, it went on for much longer too. There must have been a lot more in the area. We listened in silence, our heads down. Suddenly we heard it. The same call we had captured in Washington and a match to the bloop signature from 1997 as well. I looked at Mike, my eyes wide.

"That's not all." He said, "Listen to this."

He opened a different recording, taken from the one we had just heard but with a few voice signatures isolated and the rest silenced. He played it.

There was a back and forth, the dolphins and the bloop signature were communicating, talking to each other before the hit.

"They're communicating with each other." He beamed.

I nodded, not sure what to say. I kept listening.

We played the recording over and over again and came to the conclusion we're most likely dealing with a new dolphin like species. If this was the case and we could find proof that sonar testing was harmful to a newly discovered species, we would be able to put a stop to this kind of underwater testing.

After viewing the recording Mike had other findings he wanted to show us. We made the 45 minute journey to another facility and prepared to view the remains of an unidentified creature that had been found inside a shark. The shark had been caught in a net, and it was discovered to have puncture wounds around its mouth. In one of the wounds was a stingray barb.

I looked down at the metal table; fragments of bone and what looked like part of a collapsible ribcage as well as the end of a dolphin-like tail were laid out before me.

"So what do we have here?" I asked, already knowing what kind of answer to expect. A collapsible ribcage is common in animals that dive; the tail was obviously from a dolphin-like creature, although it seemed to have bone underneath the skin... Dolphins don't have bones in their tails...

It's the skull fragments that interest us the most, there's what seems to be a hole in the top of the head, a blowhole maybe?

We walked into the next room where a number of presentations on theories and similar findings awaited us, none of us knowing quite what to make of it all.

[Dr Mason Walsh, Marine Journal 2012]

"My name is Dr Anthony Stone and I work in land animal forensics, so was rather confused when I got the call from Dr Walsh about a newly discovered aquatic species. Nevertheless they flew me to South Africa and I agreed to look at the bone fragments they had collected. At first we thought we had found a piece of a shoulder or the base of a skull, but after some time we realised we had been looking at it upside down. After turning it we could see it was a very well formed hip bone. Along the hip was a high ridge which is most commonly found in humans, there was also a very clear iliac crest, which is designed to hold weight in creatures that walk upright. Whatever we were dealing with, at some point in its evolution it had walked upright, on two legs, like us.

We further inspected what we had been calling the tail. It looked like a dolphin's tail but was in two parts that didn't seem to fit together that well. It was also full of very thin, very delicate bones. Dolphin tails do not have bones, so this also left us with more questions than it did answers."

[Dr Anthony Stone, personal journal extract]

# Chapter Four

[Ula's story]

They call me Ula.

They say it means sea jewel. I don't feel like a jewel, I feel like a prisoner. By the land people's laws I am property of the US Navy.

They've tried to teach me things, land people concepts, like time, government and money. I don't understand any of it. They're all ridiculous notions, unintelligent and petty. I'm only just grasping using your languages. You over complicate everything.

I miss my people. I miss my home, the gentle calls of the sea creatures and the soft light that ripples through the waves and breaks the darkness. It's so bright and loud here, on land. I feel heavy just looking at it, like I'm constantly suffocating. They take me out of the water for too long, they don't realise my body is not suited for life on land anymore, they think they can make me adapt. I can't survive for longer than an hour out of the water, my internal organs would collapse. Every time they take me out they leave me close to death before putting me back in this small, awful tank. I do nothing but stare through the same glass walls every day, out into the bright, ugly lab they all sit in, studying me. I don't know how they stand it, being out there. I need the pressure of the water on my body, the feeling of floating as I drift in and out of the light, I need the space. The never ending echo's in the silence. They think this measly tank is enough, but I am dying in here. I need my family, I need the ocean.

They offered to take me back into the sea for a day on a chain once - like a dog - but only if I took them to more of my kind. Of course I refused - I wouldn't sacrifice anyone to this life of torture and imprisonment just for a day out – and I know that's what awaits my kind should the land people find them. Land people disgust me, it's hard to believe we evolved from the same species, but you can tell we did just by looking at us. I have bigger eyes, smaller ears and my nose is just two small holes in my face. My legs are fused together and my feet are formed like the end of a dolphin's tail. I have very small gills, I don't grow hair apart from a few long, fine strands on my head and I have sharp, black spikes along the back of my neck. I'm not scaly like a fish, as you thought I would be, my tail is slightly spotted like a mackerel but otherwise it's just skin, muscle and bone – like yours. My eyes are a deep red, I don't grow nails and my skin is pale white, almost fluorescent...

I'm not writing this, someone else is; a friend I made here in the facility. As well as learning how to read and write English, Spanish and Latin I learnt various dialects of sign language. I can't actually speak or use the languages I've learnt with my voice, my vocal chords aren't like yours, so I'm signing my story through my glass tank walls to the only friend I have in this place, so that maybe one day you'll come to know me and my story, and the next time you come across someone like me you'll simply observe, and then leave her be in the ocean.

When we first evolved for life in the sea our differences as men and women became apparent, while the men would often sink to the bottom of the sea and walk along the ocean floor to hunt for food, the women mostly swam like dolphins with our legs together, causing them to fuse into tails over time. This is why more women are Mermaid's while our male counterparts are usually sea apes and continue to walk on two separate legs on the sea floor, often spending small periods of time on land if it is deserted while the women are confined to the sea, unable to walk anymore. We do not interact with the land people. We've watched them change and destroy each other above us for years, we've seen their bodies fall into our caves, watched their ships sink to the ocean floor with your mothers and fathers still alive inside of them. We do not wish to be a part of your world of death and destruction.

As the mermaid and sea ape population grew, we spread, leaving Africa and travelling to new oceans, discovering new, untouched lands above the waters. Small groups of us would separate and collect once again along the shoreline, longing more and more to return to the land we once knew as home. It was very different when it hadn't been touched, a paradise - abundant with life and food. Over time these people evolved once more, regressing back into their pre-marine state. Their tails separated, their feet turned and flattened, they developed noses and grew ears, their eyes shrunk and their skin thickened and darkened with the sun, they never looked the same again. Most of us stayed away from the lands, we knew the stories of the volcanoes and earthquakes and were too afraid to go back so we stayed in the safety of the open ocean, keeping the mer-people population thriving in the darkness, away from our brothers of the land. We call them the 'changed ones'. We live in different worlds now.

My mother is beautiful, I remember her well. We all look very similar, so it's hard to explain – she looks a lot like me, only her eyes are darker, her hair is lighter and her skin is slightly browning, we get that with age. We also get smaller with age, and if we have spotted tails they darken into a deep grey or blue, my mother's is a kind of silver...

When the Navy first captured me they held me in a cage under the water for two days. They didn't realise we still need to come up for air every now and again, I had slipped into a coma when they finally pulled me up, they had to resuscitate me, using painful electrocution methods to bring me back. When I woke up I was gasping for air, but after a minute I needed the water again, being taken all the way out of the water was torture for my body, I could feel my muscles seizing, my brain going into shock... They took my thrashing for some kind of violent act against them and injected me with something that put me back to sleep. I woke up in a glass coffin like box filled with water. My head was kept still in some kind of metal clamp and my wrists and tail were shackled to the bottom. I could see these long tubes and wires poking in and out of me, one going up my nose. The room was bright; there were no ripples in the water, no movement to protect me from the harshness of it. I closed my eyes and cried, wailing and moaning to be set free, they kept me there for what seemed like eternity, studying me. I've never been so homesick in my life.

After a few days they put me in a bigger tank, it's about a mile squared and at the bottom they've put some rocks and coral. There's also a couple of fish for company, but it's nothing compared to home. It's closed off at the top so I can't escape and there's a small metal cage coming up out of the roof that I can pull myself up into when I need air.

There's always someone sitting above the tank, watching, waiting for when I pop up and documenting my movements... The walls are mostly all glass too, I can see out into their lab and they can see me. If no one is in the lab there's still camera's watching me at all times. I didn't know what they were for years, not until I learnt sign language and my friend Lucy explained them to me. Lucy is whose writing this. She's a Navy SEAL and worked in submarine rescue and experimental diving before she was made my handler a year after I came here. She is the one who taught me languages and land people concepts like relationships and jobs and photography...

I don't like the idea of relationships. They sound complicated. What if you want to move to a new part of the world but your partner doesn't want to come with you, you break up, move on, break up, move on, all for different reasons each time. We sea people spend time with whoever we're with and mate with whoever we're attracted too, of course there is jealousy, but overall we are a happy, peaceful species with no claims to each other or any other part of the land or sea. We hunt with the spears we make from wood and bone and eat when we are hungry, we take no more than we need, we are not a greedy version of our species – like you, land people.

Our friends are the dolphins and orca, the sharks hunt and eat us. We eat fish, squid, crab and other shellfish, stalking and hunting them with our spears and then feasting on their raw flesh, feeding our young and elderly first. With the squid and octopi we simply bite down on their heads to kill them, the crabs we just rip apart, they're all easy to find and kill when you know where to look.

We have different spears for different things, some for hunting, some for self-defence against sharks. I haven't hunted for food since I came here. They feed me with fish that's already been killed hours before. I crave a good hunt; I'd even take a fight with a shark over this scheduled and lonely existence.

Every morning is the same, I'm awake before the Scientists and researchers enter the lab, sometimes I hide from them amongst the rocks at the bottom of my tank. I don't always feel like being seen, the mer-people are an introverted species, myself included. I'd rather be alone forever in the emptiness of the open ocean than locked up in this tank interacting and being poked by twenty people a day.

Once I'd learnt sign language I was interrogated for information nearly every waking moment. The researchers wanted to know how we'd been existing all these years undetected, how we survived, what we ate, what we knew. They wanted to know our entire history, from the moment we broke off from the rest of the species and entered the waters up until now. I didn't know everything, but they never stopped asking, promising my freedom if I cooperated.

I'm still here.

I'm tired, I've been worked to the bone today. The Navy wants to test things like my strength and reactions, so they've been putting me through these brutal examinations. My muscles ache and I've been crying. Lucy thought you couldn't cry underwater, apparently I've proved her wrong.

I'm thinking about the day I got captured.

The last thing I remember was getting ready to migrate, we had all collected together to hunt and eat before leaving for warmer waters. I was playing with the dolphins, I was the only one of my people there, no one else had arrived yet. It was so calm, peaceful. We were all so happy...

I just remember this pain in my head, this noise. Everything hurt, it felt like someone was crushing my skull with rocks and my bones were exploding. When it stopped the pain was even worse, so much worse I couldn't move. I could feel my body seizing up, I could see the blood of my friends as it left them, coming out of their ears and eyes... I tried to stay awake but I couldn't. I thought I was going to die.

When I woke up I had washed up onto the beach. My chest felt like it was collapsing and I had no idea how long I'd been there, but I knew I didn't have long. I couldn't breathe. A land person was standing in front of me, he had poked me with a stick and ran away when he realised I

was still alive. I wish he stayed and helped me back into the water...
Maybe right now I would be with my family, hunting for a tasty squid.

I couldn't get back into the ocean, my body is too heavy for the land, I couldn't drag myself far enough. I remember trying and then collapsing through exhaustion, my body is so much heavier out of the water. The sun was burning me. I could feel my skin tightening when the Navy men came. They weren't sure what to do with me at first; they started poking at me, trying to put tubes in my throat and needles in my arms. After that they put me in their van and brought me here, putting me in that cage for two days and leaving me to drown. Stupid land people, never using their brains. Killing everything they touch.

When I was a child, I wanted to go onto the land; I wanted to see what was up there. Now I am here, I wish I never came close.

# Grandma's Secret

"Reincarnation?" I repeated back at her, trying to work out the pronunciation.

She smiled and nodded once.

"Very good." She said, continuing to dust the deep brown wooden unit that held all the placemats and cutlery for dinner.

It wasn't often I got to see my Grandma, so I was treasuring the time we had.

"I was alive before?" I asked, trying to imagine how it all worked.

"Yes, only you weren't you, you were someone else. You could have been a soldier in the war, or a cat, even."

"But how is that possible?"

She smiled.

"Everything's possible." She said very matter-of-factly. "That's how life works."

"So who were you before?" I asked as she moved onto some bookshelves, moving the books out of the way and dusting behind them.

"I've been lots of people before." She sighed happily. "Men, women, kings and queens..."

My jaw swung open in astonishment.

"You've been a king?!"

She chuckled.

"I have. I've been animals too, lions and tigers... I was even a tree once."

I stared at her in awe.

"But Grandma, how can you remember it all?"

She smiled and twitched her eyebrow, as if she was about to let me in on a big secret.

"Magic." She winked.

I rolled my eyes. She was doing that thing that grown-ups do when they think we can't understand something and so they put it down to 'magic' or 'Father Christmas'.

"Magic is not real." I said, tilting my head and looking up at her from under my raised brow.

She looked startled.

"Oh but it is." She said. "Magic is at the heart of everything we are. It's the reason we're alive and having this conversation. Without magic, your whole body would fall down dead and the world would stop turning."

I gasped at the thought.

"Is that really true?"

She nodded, her expression deadly serious.

"Oh yes. It is because of magic you're able to see and dance and speak and grow. How else would you explain it?"

I thought for a moment.

"I have no idea."

"There you are." She smiled, turning back around to face the bookshelf and moving the books and ornaments back into their rightful places.

I studied the books for a moment, noticing their titles for what was probably the first time ever; 'Grimoire for the green witch', 'the key of Solomon', 'the Egyptian Book of the Dead'...

"Grandma..." I began as she shuffled over to the coffee table, moving a small plant out of the way so that she could dust under it.

"Are you a witch?" I asked.

She smiled and winked at me in that way she always did when I was catching on to something.

"Would you like me to be?" She asked.

I thought about it for a moment. Witches where almost always the bad guys in films, but this was my Grandma – she'd never hurt me. I pictured us whizzing about the sky on her broomstick and turning people into toads. Yes, I quite liked the idea of Grandma being a witch.

I nodded and grinned.

"Oh yes Grandma, I should like that very much!"

My Grandmother chuckled and cupped my face in her hands, staring deep into my eyes as if she were sending her thoughts right into my mind.

"Come upstairs." She said. "I want to show you something."

She put her duster down on the coffee table before turning around and heading upstairs, nodding for me to follow her.

The stairs were steep, long and narrow, with a large heavy door at the top that if you weren't careful, would slam shut and chop your fingers off.

We entered her bedroom at the end of the long, dimly lit hallway.

As the door creaked open my nose was met with the smell of burning candles and incense, as if we were about to enter an old church. She smiled and flicked on the lights before blowing out the lit candles on the windowsill and turning to face me.

"People call me many things…" She began, slipping off her house shoes.

"Witch, demon, God… The mistake man makes is trying to label us, for we never fall into one category. We are a unique blend of all things, and all things are their own unique blend of us…"

She began unbuttoning her blouse.

I sat down on the bed, not knowing what to say. Slowly, she turned around to reveal her bare back.

I stared closely, noticing a thin, continuous wrinkle that travelled down the length of her spine.

"What is that?" I asked. Had she had some kind of operation?

She lifted her hair to reveal the back of her neck. I knelt up on the bed and squinted, trying to make out what she was showing me in the dim lighting. It looked like a tiny tail. Like a little mouse tail made of hair that stuck out just under her hairline.

"Pull it." She said simply.

I didn't really hesitate. I wanted to know just as much as she wanted to show me. I leant forward and reached up until my fingers pinched the end of it. It was soft and warm, more like skin than hair. I gave it a gentle tug. It came down with ease, like a warm spoon slicing through ice cream...

My eyes widened as the small tail-like thing revealed itself to be some kind of zip gliding down the length of my Grandmothers back. Her skin opened like a pencil case, but instead of a rib cage, organs and blood – I saw only black.

"Grandma..." I whispered as the zip came down further.

"Keep going." She whispered back.

I pulled it down all the way to her bottom before kneeling back down on the bed and looking up, taking in what was happening in front of me in my Grandmother's bedroom.

With a few shrugs and pulls, my Grandmother peeled off her human skin like a wet suit, stepping out of it before turning around to face me.

I couldn't help but gasp, not in shock... but awe. As her skin was opening I could see nothing but black, but now it had been removed completely the blackness became something else... alive.

I edged closer towards her, studying her new form as it ebbed and rippled like an ocean. I could see moons, stars and suns within her. Entire galaxies formed and collided where her stomach used to be, comets and meteorites flew down her shoulders and solar systems whirled in her knees. It all felt so strangely familiar.

She moved closer, sitting down on the bed beside me, the stars of her face aligning into a smile.

I reached out for what was her hand a few minutes ago, but what was now a rather accurate map of some faraway star system.

"Grandma..." I whispered, unable to manage anything else.

She reached out for me, cupping my face in her hands like she had when we were downstairs. I stared into her eyes as her hand slowly crept around to the back of my neck, feeling under my hair until her ghostly fingers clutched tightly around something I'd never felt before.

She gave it a tug.

I stared in horror as it came down...

# Ouija

Luckily, the sleepover was taking place on a Friday night otherwise Veronica's mother would have never let her go. V, as her friends called her, had just turned fourteen in March. It was now May, and her friend Natalie's birthday was just around the corner. Rightly so, a slumber party had been excitedly planned.

It was going to be the best party yet. Katie was going to steal some of her parents wine which they would secretly turn into spritzers with the Lemonade Natalie's mother provided, Lucy was going to bring some scary films from her brother's collection and Alexandra had a boom box. V was excited to spend the night with her friends. She'd never felt very accepted or popular so to be invited to the party was a huge confidence boost. She applied lashings of mascara and some pink lip gloss before she left, which made her feel very grown up indeed.

"Are you excited?" her mother smiled as they pulled up outside Natalie's mother's house.

V nodded and giggled. "I am." She said with a grin.

It had just gone 8pm and V could see the small gathering of her girlfriends through the front room window. She leaned forward to give her mother a hug before jumping out of the car, leaving a small brown teddy bear in the backseat. Her mother quickly reached behind her chair and grabbed it.

"Don't forget Papa Bear." She said, holding him out towards her daughter.

V hesitated.

"I'm fourteen mum…" She said as she climbed out of the car. "I don't think I need a teddy bear anymore…"

"Oh, okay…" Her mother replied. "Well have fun; call me if you need anything."

"I will." V smiled as she closed the door. "Love you."

"I love you too." Her mother replied as she watched her daughter from the car window. She knew Veronica would grow out of the bear sooner or later, she should have enchanted something else. A necklace perhaps… She'd never been inside Natalie's house before and she wasn't sure what kind of spirits lingered there. Sighing, she took out a small pair of scissors from her purse and wound down her window.

"Keep her sheltered, keep her safe, keep the darkness far away." She muttered as she cut some fur from the teddy bears ear. She held it in her palm a moment before blowing it out of the window and in the direction of Natalie's mother's front door, her actions unseen by her young daughter.

Inside the house, Natalie and her friends were greeting the new arrival and V promptly found herself curled up on the sofa next to Alexandra with a large glass of wine and lemonade.

By midnight the girls had finished the bottle of wine between them, watched two horror films and improvised an entire dance routine to Beyoncé's 'Crazy in love'. Natalie's parents had already gone to bed and the girls were starting to get tired.

"Shall we watch another film?" Lucy asked.

Natalie shrugged and glanced over to a small stack of board games on a shelf in the corner of the room.

"We could play a game?" She asked.

The girls all murmured sleepily between them trying to decide what to do. None of them noticed the shadow that was looming in the doorway…

"You could talk with the dead." The shadow whispered menacingly as it stepped forward into the front room, revealing itself to be Natalie's older brother, Shane.

V had never met him before and instantly the hairs on her arm stood to attention, wary of the sudden change in atmosphere. There was something terribly dark about him. Something she wasn't sure the others could sense.

"How do you talk with the dead?" Alexandra asked, intrigued by his obscure suggestion.

V knew how. She'd seen her mother do it plenty of times. As a witch, talking with spirits was a daily activity – but she wasn't sure if that was something she'd be interested in doing herself, after all, she was still very young and not nearly half as knowledgeable about these things as her mother.

"Make a Ouija board." Shane replied simply. "It's easy, just draw it out on a piece of paper and use a tumbler for a planchette."

'Wrong.' Thought V. 'That's wrong. Where are the offerings? The circle of protection?' Shane had absolutely no idea what he was talking about.

"Can you show us?" Natalie asked.

Shane's smile made V uncomfortable.

"Of course." He said, walking out of the room to get some paper, pens and a tumbler.

The girls all squealed excitedly, the horror movies earlier had clearly made quite an impression, V wasn't as impressed.

"Should we really be doing this?" She asked nervously.

"Why not?" Lucy asked, wondering why anyone would object to such an interesting activity.

"I mean… we don't know what might come through."

"Makes it more exciting, doesn't it?" Alexandra giggled.

V decided to keep quiet; she valued her social circle and didn't want to be left out or labelled a bore.

Within the minute, Shane was back and sitting crossed legged at the coffee table, scribbling away on a piece of large paper.

Slowly, the girls gathered around him to peer over his shoulder at what he was doing. The paper had been neatly decorated with all the letters of the alphabet, numbers 0-9, 'Yes', 'no' and 'Goodbye'.

'This isn't right.' V thought to herself nervously. She wondered what her mother would say if she was here, she'd probably rip up the paper and tell Shane off for being so stupid before giving him a lecture on demonology...

"Ready?" Shane asked as he turned the tumble upside down and placed it in the middle of the paper.

The girls all nodded excitedly. V didn't.

"Shouldn't we light a white candle?" She asked.

"Why?" Shane raised an eyebrow, clearly unfamiliar with the practices he was trying to replicate.

"For protection." V answered simply.

Shane scoffed and ignored V's suggestion as he placed two fingers onto the tumbler and gestured at the girls to do the same.


Back at home, Veronica's mother sat at a small round table shuffling an old deck of tarot cards. She knew something wasn't right, she could feel the shift in her daughters energy, even from afar.

"Go to her." A disembodied voice whispered. "She needs you, Isla. The child is in danger..."

Isla clutched the crystal necklace around her neck and took a deep breath as she spread the cards over the table.

"What's happening, uncle?" she asked the voice as a ghostly hand rested on her shoulder comfortingly.

The voice didn't respond.

Isla ran her fingertips over the top of the cards until she felt a pull towards one. She quickly turned it over, then another, then another.

The Devil.

The Tower.

Death.

Isla froze. She'd never seen a reading like it before, whatever was happening at that sleepover was about to take a dark turn.

Quickly, Isla gathered some herbs and salt, mixing them together and using them to draw a large circle on the wooden floor of her front room. She lit some white and purple candles, placing them around her as the ghost of her Uncle Jack stepped into view.

"Take me to her." Isla whispered as she sat down in the middle of the circle and closed her eyes. Almost instantly, Isla's spirit was transported out of her body and to the spot she had parked in just hours earlier outside of Natalie's parent's house.

She looked around at the ghostly sprits that were now surrounding the house. Unbeknown to the teenagers, calling out to the spirit world is like holding up a dead gazelle to a pride of lions, and the lions were closing in.


Back at the sleepover, the tumbler had begun to move.

"Who is with us?" Shane asked.

The tumbler shook gently before moving across the board.

F-R-I-E-N-D-S

The girls looked nervously at one another, unsure of what to think.

"How did you die?" Shane asked

N-O-T-D-E-A-D

The tumbler spelt.

S-O-M-E-W-H-E-R-E-E-L-S-E

"I don't like this." Natalie whispered, not moving her fingers from the tumbler. "What if it's a demon?"

"Demons aren't real." Shane answered.

V raised an eyebrow.

"Where are you?" Shane asked the spirit.

There was a pause before the tumbler moved again.

B-E-H-I-N-D-Y-O-U

The group all looked nervously over their shoulders, including V who for a minute, could swear she saw her mother's face in the window...

Isla frowned from outside the house. She wasn't disappointed in the teenagers for messing about with such things, she was more disappointed in herself for not being more open with her daughter about the dangers.

"Help me Uncle." Isla whispered as she studied her daughters face, noticing how uncomfortable she looked. They would have to have a conversation about saying 'no' when this is all over.

Uncle Jack looked to his left and whistled, chuckling to himself happily as a little white dog with a brown patch over its eye came running towards them from down the road.

Isla gasped, recognizing the pup instantly.

"Manolo." She smiled as he came bounding towards her, jumping into her arms and attempting to lick her face with his cold breeze of a ghostly tongue.

Isla giggled. It had been a long time since she'd seen him.

Uncle Jack turned towards the house, nodding at his young niece on the other side of the window.

He patted the dogs head, reminding him he had work to do.


"What do you want?" Shane asked the makeshift Ouija board as a cold breeze entered the room.

V recognized it instantly as it ran under the table and brushed against her leg.

"What was that?" Alexandra whispered, feeling the same presence.

V said nothing.

The tumbler didn't move.

"Do you have a message for us?" Shane asked, his voice a little louder this time.

G-O-T-O-B-E-D

The tumbler spelt out.

The girls giggled nervously.

"No." Shane laughed.

Suddenly, the tumbler flew across the room, smashing against the wall.

"A bit much, don't you think?" Uncle Jack asked, a slight chuckle in his voice.

Isla shrugged as she flipped the make shift Ouija board onto the floor, causing the girls to scream and scarper to their bedrooms.

"They need to learn."

# Denny

My name is Denny. I think it was Dennis originally but I don't really remember details like that. I was liberated from my birthing planet as a child. I don't have a lot of memories from that time apart from my father. I think that's because I was with him the night I was taken, they left him there though. He's probably dead by now.

I'd say it's been around 50 - 60 Earth years since then. So I should be in my 70's now, but time is different up here and I've aged much slower than I would have had I stayed. I don't really look like I'm out of my 20's yet. The first real memory I have is of being on board the DSV, which stands for deep space vehicle. I had been put into hibernation for about 8 years and when I woke up we were just outside the MACS galaxy, specifically; MACS0647-JD.

A small planet we call Yunur became my new home, and it was a home I loved from the second I saw it. It was an Earth-like planet and nature seemed to act relatively similar as back home; we had trees, lakes, animals and mountains, but it was better in a way Earthly words cannot begin to describe.

The first thing I saw when I got off the DSV was a large airbase, with over 1000 ships both bigger and smaller than the one I had been on, beyond that were mountains, rivers and valleys. The sky was hues of lilac and the grass tones of turquoise. The trees were over a thousand feet high and looked like giant mushrooms; it was quite the sight for my young eyes. The colours were fantastic, bolder and brighter than Earth could ever know.

As I grew up I learnt about their technology. I worked as an engineer on the DSV's for a good few years, learning about how they worked and how to build and fix them. They travel by latching on to nearby planets gravitational pulls and then using that force to propel themselves through space. Once I had graduated I was given a place to live. Here we call them 'units' but they're basically just large apartments that can be stacked on top of each other to create huge structures of any design. Everyone is given one once they have graduated – to graduate just means that you've shown you are able to live independently and can contribute to the society. Before I got my unit I lived in a small base at the training centre, which is where we learn the way of our people. Each day began with chanting and exercise, which I found strange at first, but after a while I found it had a dramatic impact on the way I functioned – I was calmer, more focused and felt stronger both physically and mentally. After that we worked on the vehicles, then farmed and prepared food before returning to our units to change, meditate or socialize if we chose.

In my small community there are about 8,000 people. A few that I've met are from Earth but mostly they are from other galaxies and planets I'd never heard of. We were all given headsets that translated the different languages for us so that we could understand each other and make friends. There was no religion, no war and no disease. We all ate the same diet, which was specially designed to properly sustain our bodies. You see, although we all came from other planets and spoke other languages, we are all some form of humanoid, and we all had the same basic needs.

"How?" You ask...

Well, it turns out the planets weren't populated organically. Each planet is actually a farm for different types of humanoid. The Yunurs (among others) travel all over the multiverse farming humans for one specific purpose; our survival. Once the population reaches optimum level and the people have evolved as much as they can, the Yunurs return to test and choose a select few humans to become the leaders of the next 'farm' and breed of humanoid. Which is how the story of Adam and Eve came to be on Earth I guess; we were trying to romanticize our roots.

The Yunurs choose exactly 3,000 of the finest humans from all different planets to start a new farm, staying with them for the first 10,000 years to help them build societies and learn about their new home. This is called the adjustment period. As the world becomes more and more populated, the different races mix together and change to align with the planet, we call this evolution. Depending on the conditions of the planet, their hair, eye and skin colour may change; bone structure and height can also be affected. It's also not uncommon for people to grow new limbs and organs. In fact one of my closest friends has two hearts, three stomachs and is 8 feet tall. This process over time creates new races of human the multiverse has never seen before – our job is to cross breed the species in an attempt to create the ultimate human race using the best of the best.

By the time this message reaches Earth, the people may all be dead. I'm hoping they're not, and that maybe someone reading this knows of my father and would leave some flowers at his grave for me, but I've been told not to get my hopes up.

It is said the planet I'm from is one of the worst in human history, and human history goes way back before Earth ever came to be. We messed up bad, and I mean REAL bad. Never on any farm has a species been so violent and greedy. I didn't know as a boy the true state of the planet I lived on, my father did well to shelter me from the horrors of the world around me – but as a man growing up on Yunur I have learnt more about my home planet than the current inhabitants could ever wish to comprehend. The technology here is far more advanced than Earth can ever know; we have many satellites around your planet and can watch any part of the world, any person, at any time. The way you live saddens me, scares me. The DNA that went into creating the Earthly humans was a dangerous and catastrophic mix of genetics that clashed with fury. Thankfully, records are well kept here and we can be sure the same mistake won't be made twice.

Why are you so intent on destroying yourselves? Destroying the world around you? You've forgotten who and what you are.

One of our jobs here is to watch the humans via our satellites to see if anyone is worthy of helping build the new races. If they are deemed fit for judgement a small team will travel to that planet, bring the human on board the ship and place a small implant under their skin which will take readings of their physical strengths and weaknesses to see if their DNA is suitable for creating a healthy, mentally stable race of people. I am told this is why my father was not brought with me; he had a heart condition. I don't carry the same genome and so was deemed healthy and intelligent enough to reproduce successfully.

Soon, it will be my turn to start a new race. Whilst we live on Yunur we don't breed. We are sterilized as soon as we arrive and the sterilization ends when it is our time to populate a new planet. Yunur is a base planet, not a breeding planet – that is what the farms are for.

I hope I will be a good father. I hope the knowledge I place in my children will not be lost, warped or told in vain, like it was on Earth. We have been told to leave instructions for the future generations, the ones we won't be around for, letters in stone that won't erode or be lost in time, hidden messages to guide them. I'm looking forward to that part, a friend and I have spoken about building large statues and pyramids marking the star systems they come from, a way to honour our past I guess.

I do wish things could be different. If I could I would come back to Earth in a heartbeat and show the humans how to fix things, but it would be a futile mission. They have caused far too much damage to their poor mother planet, sucking her dry of her resources, poisoning the oceans and air, abusing their minds and bodies. The Earthly people are a sick and dying breed, and as much as I wish to fix them, I know I cannot. I wish it wasn't so, but the sooner my people die out the better things will be for the other inhabitants of my home planet. I'm sorry father, wherever you may be.

We don't use money here, we don't value material things. We value our strength as a community, our roles in supporting each other and having a comfortable and happy life. We value a good physical and mental state. We do things so that our species can thrive – it is not a competition of who can get the richest, most famous or be the best looking, as it is on Earth. How strange you are to us.

If anyone is reading this right now, if my message has somehow reached Earth before my people have left it or passed on – I implore you to change your ways. Rethink your laws and belief systems. Do things for the love and care of your species. Instead of believing in and fighting over an invisible God – believe in yourselves, fight for the visible and measurable planet around you. Do what is right, not what temporarily masks the pain you know you are all in.

I promise I will do better in the next world, for you.

Make peace with your Gods brothers, your time is near.

# Mermaids

My name is Noah.

My mother died just after I was born and my father re-married quickly. I don't really remember much of my step-mother; I didn't really spend much time with her at all. Whenever she came around I was sent to play in my bedroom. She had her own children, they stayed with her.

I remember that night though, she came into my bedroom when the sky was black and the moon was full. I hadn't been asleep; I'd been staring at it through the window. The house was silent as we put on our coats and left quietly through the back door. She told me there was something she needed my help with. I don't know what I thought was going to happen, but I did as I was told.

She took my father's car and we drove towards the beach. She didn't say anything on the journey, apart from whenever she saw another car on the road and she told me to get down... It was strange but I didn't question it.

When we got to the beach she got out before me and had a cigarette. She seemed sad, but I didn't know why. She told me to get out of the car and we walked onto the sand, past the ice cream place and into the caves. She told me to sit down and wait for her, not to move until she got back. She made me promise.

I stayed there for as long as I could, but after a few hours I figured she wasn't coming back for me. I was worried at first, worried she'd gotten hurt or lost – but soon that worry turned to sadness as I realized the awful truth. She'd left me here on purpose. She'd always wanted rid of me. I decided to try and find my way home. We didn't live to far from the beach and I'd made the journey hundreds of times before. Surely I'd be able to work it out...

My dad met my step-mother when I was about four. I've never really liked her, and I knew she always treated me different, but I never thought she'd just leave me somewhere. I sighed and stood up, ready to make the journey home.

As I started to leave the cave and head back to the main road, I heard a strange singing. It wasn't anything in English and it didn't sound like a normal person's voice either, it was much too high and shaky and delicate...

I crept to the edge of the cave to find the source of the mysterious singing.

"Hello?" I called, looking around the outside of the cave. The strange voice went silent.

"Please help me." I whispered. I was frightened, but relieved that an adult was nearby to help.

"I'm all alone..."

There wasn't a reply for at least a minute. I began to think that whoever was singing had walked away, but finally, just before I was about to turn and leave – it came again.

"Come closer..." The voice whispered.

I walked forward nervously, realizing I couldn't see whoever it was that I was talking to. They weren't standing in front of me as I'd expected them to be. I looked around, confused before noticing the upper half of a young woman's body in the water.

"H...hello." I whispered, I couldn't manage any more than that, I was frightened.

"Hello." She whispered back, staring at me with these huge, pale green eyes. She didn't seem to be wearing anything.

"Was it you... singing?" I asked, moving towards her.

She nodded.

"Why are you here?" She asked.

I sat down on the rocks, digging my heels in to the sand.

"My step-mother left me." I replied with a shrug, trying hard not to cry.

She swam forward, touching her hand to my bare knee.

"That's so sad…" She said. "Left you all alone?"

I nodded, my eyes finally flooding with tears. "She hates me."

She tilted her head in sympathy.

"Horrible, nasty woman." She said.

I agreed sadly. "Yes, I wish my own mother were still here…"

The strange woman looked at me with tears in her eyes and squeezed my arm gently, trying to be comforting.

"Where is she?" She asked quietly.

I told her what happened… She cried a little, it was weird. She asked to be my friend.

"You want to be my friend?" I asked her, wondering why, no one really wanted to be my friend. I only had one friend at school. Everyone else thought I was weird.

She nodded and held out a pale hand.

"Come with me." She whispered.

I looked at her, wondering where we would go…

"I'll keep you safe." She said.

I nodded and took a step closer, reaching out for her small, wet hand. It was comforting to be in her presence. I know I had only just met her, but I felt happier around her than I did in my own home, with my own family.

She smiled as our skin touched and led me deeper into the water.

"Here, come with me… Don't be afraid, the waves aren't too bad here… That's it, take my hand and I'll guide you…" She spoke softly, putting me on to her back and swimming out to sea. Her skin was so pale I could almost see through it. Her bones jutted out and her hair was long and fine like strands of silk…

"Hold on tightly…" She shouted at me over the noise of the waves and wind… My knuckles felt like blocks of ice as I gripped hold of her tightly and clung to her body, she was freezing.

"You'll get used to it." She smiled, as if reading my thoughts. She was right, I did. You will too.

What did you say your name was, Ursula? That's a beautiful name.

We kept swimming until I could no longer see the cave I met you in, see how it gets smaller the further out we go? The water's up to our knees now...

Let's keep walking until it's at our necks.

As the cave disappeared, she told me to hold my breath and swam downwards. I remember the pressure of the water getting heavier and heavier as my lungs begged me for air. Have you ever been submerged? No? It's a scary feeling... Your ears begin to ring when you can't take anymore and you become confused...

"Not much longer now... Hold on..." She whispered, swimming faster towards what looked like a hole in the ocean floor.

Here, the sea is at our tummies now. Doesn't it feel nice once you get used to how cold it is?

I don't remember swimming into the hole, I think that was the moment I died. The next thing I knew I was back in the cave and it was a year later. I knew because someone had left a newspaper behind, it was 1983, and there was no mention of me or what had happened.

Once it got dark Ula came back for me – that's her name, the mermaid. It's a bit like Ursula isn't it? How funny.

She put me on her back as she had done that night exactly one year before and we swam out to sea. I watched the cave until I could no longer see it, just like I had done the first time.

"Hold your breath..." Ula said, like she had before.

I took the deepest breath I could and held it, but alas, as we got closer to the hole everything went black, just as it had the first time and I woke up again a year later, only to repeat the same thing. The year after that the same thing happened, as it did the year after that. I'm not sure what year it is now... 1993 you say? How peculiar, I've been here a while. The sea is at our chins now, can you smell the salt? Imagine what it would feel like to come close to drowning, would you like to try it?

Here, just dip your head under the water like this... now let's stay here for as long as we can.

1, 2, 3... can you feel your chest getting tight? 4, 5, 6... Let me hold you here so you don't drift up for air by mistake. There... It's scary isn't it, I can tell by the way your eyes just snapped open and you're staring at me. Would you like to go up for air? You can't yet. They say the human brain only starts shutting down after a few minutes without air... Stop struggling. Ula would love to meet you.

Besides... I need a friend...

# The Devils Mask

I grew up listening to the stories about it; 'The Devils Mask'. It was made by an old shaman who practiced dark magic. It was my tribe the shaman belonged to, my people he killed. My grandfather himself was only young at the time, and his father had been one of the Shamans victims.

The Shaman wasn't always evil, he used to be a healer, curing people of their ailments and troubled sleep, but as the years dragged on he found people were no longer grateful or appreciative of his work. They cared not for the energy it took of him; only what they could gain. The Shaman grew increasingly angry and hateful of his tribe, the people that had once honoured him and turned to him for guidance had taken advantage of his powers and given nothing in return. So one night, whilst wandering the spirit realm, he summoned a powerful dark spirit.

No one knows exactly what it was that he summoned, some say a demon, others say it was the devil himself, all anyone remembers is the foul smelling smoke from the fire he burnt that night. The next day, his first victim was claimed.

Talking Water, a young boy of only 14 years old disappeared without a trace. Everyone knew who it was, but nobody had any proof. A week after that, a woman vanished in a similar manor. One moment she was there, the next she had gone. Nobody ever saw her again. This pattern of weekly mysterious disappearances continued for a while, until eventually the tribe couldn't take anymore. Even without any evidence; all fingers pointed towards the Shaman, and he was sentenced to death by fire.

The Shaman didn't try to run. He didn't shy away from his punishment. Instead, when the sentence was read out to him, he smiled.

On the day of his death the Shaman appeared wearing a mask. It was in the face of a horrifying monster, with twisted features and a fearsome expression. He said the mask had been forged from the skin and bones of his victims, including little Talking Water. After admitting his crimes he told the people that he would gladly burn for what he had done, but should the people kill him they will be met with a great curse that will affect their bloodline for all of eternity.

The Shamans sentence was carried out and he was burnt shortly after his speech, but the next day, when the ash from the fire was being cleared; the mask was found; intact.

The mask was buried along with all of the Shamans belongings, but not long after, misery and misfortune befell the tribe in the form of famine, disease and death.

It was decided the mask would be dug up and destroyed, however no matter what they did; the mask remained as though untouched.

A young man by the name of Grey Bird volunteered to take the mask far away from the tribe, saying he would find someone to cast the spirit back into the other realm where it belonged.

But that's not what happened.

The tribe didn't know it, but Grey Bird had his own plans. He took the mask into a nearby town and sold it, leaving with the money he'd made. No one ever saw him again.

Over time, things seemed to return to normal. Everyone believed the mask had been destroyed and the curse lifted and tried to put the ordeal at the back of their minds. Until one day when a woman visited the tribe, inquiring about a mask that looked like it had been made from skin...

She said her family had been gifted the mask from a friend who had since passed away in a terrible accident. After the passing, the girl had been plagued with a series of horrifying dreams and visions, leading her here. Some men went with her to retrieve the mask and release her of the curse, but when they arrived the entire house had been burnt to the ground with her family inside. The mask was never found, but we know it's out there, somewhere close by. My father and I have been tracing it for the past twenty years, but every time we get close to finding it, it disappears without a trace, leaving behind nothing but a pile of ash.

The last place we tracked it to was a charity shop just around the corner from you, which I guess is why I'm writing you this letter. Don't be alarmed, we're on our way, but it might be sometime before we get there. If you see a mask for sale; don't buy it. Don't touch it, and if it tries to talk to you, don't listen.

Just run.

# The Thing in my Daughter's Bedroom

I've rented places my whole adult life but a few months ago I had finally saved enough to buy somewhere. My daughter and I spent weeks viewing places and checking out the local schools and parks until eventually we settled on a little cottage in Wilsborough.

For the first month or so everything was perfect. The house came with an office and studio space so I worked a lot from home. My daughter had a lovely play room and so her evenings were mostly spent in there, painting or playing with her toys.

Around six weeks ago my daughter started waking up during the night and getting into bed with me, sometimes I didn't even hear her get up – I'd just wake up in the morning and there she was.

Now, my daughters always been very independent, she was sleeping in her own room from 3 months old and has always slept throughout the night without problem, so to me – her behavior was bordering on strange. I shrugged it off as just 'only child' anxieties and thought it would pass, but if anything it got worse.

After a few weeks she wouldn't even go into her room once bedtime came around, she'd get straight into my bed and no matter what I said she was adamant that's where she needed to be. Again; I shrugged it off. 'Maybe the move has been stressful for her.' I thought.

About a week ago I woke up to her talking in her sleep.

"It's still there... It's still there..." She mumbled. I cuddled up to her and stroked her hair until she stopped.

A few days later it happened again.

"It's still there..."

And then again the night after that.

"It's still there..."

"What is, sweetie?" I asked.

"The thing in my room…" She mumbled before falling back into a soundless slumber.

I shuddered, it was a weird thing for her to say in her sleep – especially for a little girl who's never talked in her sleep before, but I shrugged it off as some kind of recurring nightmare and wrapped my arms around her tightly.

The next morning was a Monday. After breakfast we headed back upstairs to clean our teeth and get ready when I noticed she would no longer even step foot in her bedroom, not even to get clothes.

"What is it baby?" I asked as I stepped past her and took her uniform out of her cupboard. She didn't answer, instead she just stared at something behind me from the doorway. I turned around but there was nothing there.

I held out my hand. "Come here." I said gently. "Help me find you some socks."

She shook her head and backed away. She looked terrified.

I finished getting her clothes together and took her into my room to get dressed.

"Is everything ok?" I asked.

She nodded, clearly not ready to talk about whatever it was that was disturbing her.

"You know you can talk to me about anything, right?" I asked.

She nodded, looking nervously towards my doorway.

That night the same thing happened, as soon as she cleaned her teeth she ran straight in my room. I decided to test the waters a bit…

"Do you want to come with me to get your pyjamas?" I asked.

"No. I'll just sleep naked." She replied quickly.

"You can't sleep naked it's the middle of winter." I laughed. "Come on. I'll hold your hand."

She shook her head.

I frowned, not understanding what it was that she was so afraid of.

"It's still there…" She whispered.

I froze. That's what she'd being saying in her sleep…

"What is?" I asked.

She shrugged, not knowing what to say – but her face said it all.

"The thing…" She answered.

"Do you want to show me where it is and I'll get rid of it?" I asked, thinking it's probably just a spider or even a pile of toys that looked like a scary face in the dark…

She nodded, taking my hand and walking with me to her bedroom door. She wouldn't come inside the room, but she stood at the doorway and pointed to a spot near her bed.

"It's there…" She whispered, moving to hide behind the door frame.

I turned on the light and looked around.

"There's nothing here baby." I said, walking into the room. Suddenly a cold shiver ran down my spine and my stomach turned as I felt a cold, heavy hand rest upon my right shoulder…

"It's behind you…" She whispered.

# Boy in the Window

"There's a boy in the window." My wife said, pointing across our garden to the house opposite.

I looked at where she was pointing.

She was right, in the top right hand window of the house opposite was a small boy, probably no older than 10. He was looking in our direction but I don't think he saw us.

We'd lived here for a good six years now and never seen any children around, it was a small road, one of those cul-de-sacs where everyone knows everyone and pretty much all the occupants where old couples.

"Maybe he's visiting?" I replied with a shrug.

She nodded, accepting the possibility he could just be someone's grandson. We went to bed shortly after. The next morning my wife was in a baking mood and I woke up to the smell of brownies – which I'm always happy to do.

"What's the occasion?" I asked, kissing her cheek as she cleaned up the kitchen.

"No occasion, I just thought I'd take some brownies around for that little boy, I saw him in the window again this morning." She smiled.

I smiled back, her kindness was one of the reasons I fell in love with her. She was always doing something for someone, even people she didn't know.

"Great, I'll come with you." I said.

We got dressed and headed round while the brownies were still warm. My wife rang the doorbell.

No answer.

"Maybe they're not home?" I shrugged.

"They must be... I saw the boy at the window again just before we left."

I shrugged again, "Maybe he got in the bath or something?"

She didn't buy it. We stood there for at least another three minutes ringing the bell and tapping gently on the windows. In the end we decided to just come back a bit later.

"Well, they taste good if that's any consolation." I said, shoving an entire brownie in my mouth.

"You're so greedy." She giggled.

When we got home my wife headed straight to the kitchen to put the brownies in a cake box so they stayed fresh.

"Look, he's right there!" She shouted, just as I'd sat down.

"Who?" I asked, momentarily forgetting who we'd just been talking about.

"The boy!" She shouted back. "Come and look!"

I groaned, not wanting to get back up now I'd sat down, but I stood up anyway and went to look.

"Right there!" She said, pointing.

"I don't see him..." I replied, looking towards the top right hand window.

"Not there, look he's in the left window now."

I looked to the window on the left and sure enough, there he was. His mouth was moving as if he was speaking to someone, only his eyes were looking directly at my wife.

"Well... What do you know." Was all I could say.

"Do you want to take the brownies round again?"

She didn't answer me for a few seconds, she was just staring at him, as if hearing what he was saying. Slowly she nodded.

"Yes... Let's take the brownies again." She said, still not taking her eyes away from his.

I frowned, she was acting a bit strange. I waved a hand in front of her face.

"Hello? Earth to Erica?" I laughed, trying to get her to look away.

"Oh stop it." She snapped, turning to pick up the brownies. "You stay here I'll take them."

I raised an eyebrow. "Are you sure?"

She didn't answer, instead she simply pushed passed me and left. Had I annoyed her somehow? I wasn't sure what I'd done. I decided to stay in the kitchen and watch the window to see what happened. A few minutes later my wife appeared at the window, next to the boy.

I smiled and waved at them both, watching them eat a brownie each. My wife waved half-heartedly before turning to face the boy, who didn't acknowledge me at all. She looked as if she was crying. Worried and confused, I took out my phone and looked at them both through the camera, zooming in so I could get a better look. She was definitely crying, but why? I had no idea... It looked like she was shaking with fear, as if the little boy had just told her the most horrifying news...

I decided to go round there and make sure everything was ok.

I ran round quickly, with all the worst possible scenarios playing in my head. Had she found a dead body? Was the boy being neglected? Why was she crying? She only went round there a few minutes ago...

I reached the house quickly and rang the doorbell.

No answer.

"Hello?" I called through the letterbox.

Still no answer.

Surely my wife had heard me, why wasn't she answering the door?

"Erica!" I shouted through the letterbox again, starting to worry. What on Earth was going on?

"Erica!"

Still no answer. I decided to try the next door neighbour; it was the kind of village where everyone gave a spare key to their neighbour. A young woman answered.

"Hi, sorry to disturb you but do you by any chance have a key for next door? I think somethings happened..."

The woman frowned, looking confused.

"I didn't think anyone lives there." She said.

I looked back at the house, noticing for the first time how run down it was, how the net curtains behind the windows were all torn and grey.

"My wife took them brownies…" I said, not quite knowing how to finish my sentence.

"Sorry…" She replied. "Have you tried the side door?"

"Side door?"

She nodded. "There's a little door down the side of the house, maybe they're in the kitchen and can't hear the bell?"

I nodded. The majority of people who lived around here were old and had hearing problems, it wouldn't surprise me. I took her advice and walked down the side of the house.

There was a door alright, but it was boarded up. I knocked on it anyway.

"Hello?" I called.

Still nothing.

I was starting to panic. Where the hell was my wife? Why wasn't she answering me?

I ran back around to the front of the house and opened the letterbox again.

"Erica!" I yelled through it.

"James…" A faint voice replied.

"Open the door!" I yelled back.

Her voice didn't come again. I ran back to the neighbour's house and banged on her door, this time her husband answered.

"Hey." He said, looking around and wondering what all the yelling was about.

"Call the police, please… Something's happened to my wife."

The man didn't ask questions, I think he could sense the urgency in my voice. He headed inside and came back a few moments later with a phone pressed to his ear.

"Police please…" He said as his wife came to the door.

"What's going on?" She asked.

"I don't know…"

I didn't either.

I went back to the house and began banging on all the windows again, the couple from next door came and stood outside, watching me, wondering what the hell was going on. I must have looked crazy.

"Police are on their way." The man yelled as I ran back down the side of the house. I climbed the fence and dropped down into the back garden, looking up at the top left window. No one was there.

"Erica!" I yelled again.

Suddenly a little face appeared at the window, it was the boy. He raised a finger to his lips as if telling me to be quiet.

"Where is she?" I called. He didn't answer.

I started kicking at the back door, hoping the fear of it breaking would get someone to come and open it. No one came.

A minute later I heard police sirens. I jumped back over the fence and ran to the front of the house.

"What's going on?" The first officer asked as he stepped out of the car.

"My wife... Somethings happened to my wife, she's in that house but no one will let me in."

The second officer rang the doorbell.

"Hello?" He called. "It's the police, open the door."

No answer.

He tried again, still nothing.

"Do you know if anyone has a spare key or?" He asked me.

I shook my head. "I've already asked."

"Ok, no worries." He took a step back. "Shall we kick it down?" He asked the first officer, who looked at me.

"Do you think her life is in danger?" He asked.

"YES!" I yelled, now in full panic mode.

The officer raised his hands in a 'calm down' kind of way.

"Ok..." He said, "Don't worry we'll get this sorted. Step back please..."

I took a few steps back as the officer took something out the boot of their car and used it to smash the door down.

"Jesus Christ…" The woman from next door whispered from behind me as a foul stench drifted out from the house and hit us all. "What the hell is that?"

I stepped forward as the officers entered the house.

"Hello?" I heard one of them call. "Is anyone home?"

Just seconds after the officers crossed the threshold they both ran back outside heaving, their eyes watering from the odour.

"What?" I yelled. "What's happening?"

"Stay here please." One of the officers said, holding me back with one hand as he used the other to try and stop himself vomiting.

"No my wife is in there…. Erica?!" I shouted as loud as I could. Still, no reply came.

"Sir… Please."

I stepped back as the officers re-entered the building, covering their noses with hankie chiefs.

The smell was like rotting food and as I looked into the house I could see flies and maggots covering nearly every surface.

"What the hell is going on?" I whispered.

The woman from next door stepped forward and touched my arm.

"Are you ok?" She asked.

I shook my head, not knowing what to do or say.

We watched the officers head up the staircase, which had clearly been rotting away for years.

"Hello?" They called. "Is anyone here?"

Still nothing.

My panic level rose once more and I ran in after them without thinking, knowing there was something horribly wrong. I didn't know what, but something had happened to my wife and I needed to be there.

"Sir, please…" One of the officers began as I followed them up the stairs.

"No." I replied, more stern than I planned on being. "She's my wife…"

The officers nodded, too focused on preventing themselves from vomiting to follow any sort of protocol.

"She was in here…" I said, pointing to a bedroom opposite the staircase, the one I'd seen her in through the window.

"Ok, stay here. We'll go check it out."

I nodded, waiting by the stairs for my wife's voice.

"Jesus…" I heard one of the officers say as the other one heaved.

I began walking towards the bedroom, not knowing what I was about to find.

"What is it?" I called.

"Stay back!" One of them yelled, "Do NOT come in here, wait outside, please!"

I shook my head and walked in after them, 'not a chance in hell' I thought.

I entered the room and froze.

There, on the double bed was my wife, curled up with a little boy – no older than ten. Their eyes were both open and staring at each other. Cobwebs covered their bodies and the yellow summer dress my wife had on earlier that morning was faded and covered in filth.

They looked like they'd been dead for twenty years.

"No…" I whispered.

The officers looked at me.

"Is this your wife?" They asked.

I couldn't answer. I sank to the floor shaking as one of the officers noticed a plate on the windowsill.

A plate of freshly baked brownies…

# The Vampires Child

Her name was Emily, but her father only ever called her 'child'. It was something she had simply learned to accept, even recognizing it as a term of endearment. Her mother had died soon after she was born and her father was getting old, so he hired me to help care for them both.

I started working for them in June 1995 and moved in permanently soon after. The house was old, Victorian and crumbling with poison ivy growing up the side. The front door was black, as was most of the interior. Viktor was not a very colourful man, but even though the house lacked colour it was still immaculately decorated in shades of grey. There were no mirrors, and Viktor was quite against having them in the house or around Emily. I didn't understand why but I didn't question him, he was paying me a lot of money. After the first few weeks I just got used to checking my reflection in the windows and all thoughts of mirrors left my head. Emily was a bright child, independent and emotionally developed. Her mind was like that of a young woman rather than a child and we quickly became close. She became like a daughter to me within the first year, and I wouldn't have had it any other way.

Viktor never wanted Emily to see him weak and so spent the last year or so of his life in the basement, avoiding her gaze and hiding his dark sunken eyes behind sunglasses when he was up and about. He always wore a large black cloak that was lined with vibrant red velvet – the only colour I ever saw him wear. I assumed it was to hide his deteriorating figure but I later learned he'd worn one for most of his life, in fact Emily had never seen him without one.

During the last few weeks of his life he could barely move. He became more confused and weary by the day. We knew it wouldn't be long before it was his time to go...

We began to discuss things like his will and what would happen to Emily after he was gone, things he'd never really spoken to me about before. He asked me to stay with her, to watch over her and look after her until she was old enough to care for herself. Of course I promised I would, I wouldn't have left her even if he hadn't asked me to stay, I'd grown to love her too much.

"She's a special child..." He whispered to me as I fed him supper one night.

"She is." I smiled and nodded in agreement.

"Now open wide."

He pushed my hand away and stared at me in a way that still haunts me even now.

"No... You don't understand." He whispered in a deep and serious tone. "She is different to the rest of them. She has... certain needs."

I frowned slightly and nodded at him to continue, not quite sure of what he meant.

He glanced behind me weakly, making sure she wasn't listening from the doorway.

"Our kind are not like yours."

I leaned in closer, realizing by the tone of his voice that what he was trying to tell me was rather serious.

"The child... she has..." He exhaled loudly and closed his eyes, as if trying to explain himself had exhausted him completely.

I smiled sympathetically and tried to encourage him to finish eating but he pushed my hand away a second time, shaking his head.

"Listen..." He whispered, placing a pale and heavily wrinkled hand on my arm. "When I am gone, you are all she has. You need to know what she needs..."

"I'm listening." I replied, placing my hand on his.

"Your kind has a name for us, but it is not what we call ourselves. Over time we have evolved to live like our human cousins, but we are not the same. We still have certain... unfashionable requirements to live a full life..."

I took a tissue from my pocket and wiped the beads of sweat that were beginning to form on his forehead, brushing his thinning, jet black hair away from his face.

There was a pause before I sighed and responded quietly.

"I know." I smiled sadly. I think I knew from the minute I met them both, there had always been something very different about them, they weren't like anyone I'd ever met; man or child.

"You know?" He asked.

I nodded.

"How?"

"Well, the fact there's no mirrors in the house was my first guess." I whispered, chuckling softly.

He smiled back. I guess he was relieved he didn't have to finish explaining himself.

"So, you know what we are..." He nodded, confirming it to himself. "And, you're ok with it?"

"Ok with you being... mythological?" I asked, not quite ready to use the word 'vampire' in case he found it offensive. He laughed at my choice of wording before looking down at our hands sadly.

"It is a curse as much as it is a blessing. Our minds have evolved to be above the beasts we were, but sadly our diets have remained similar to the ancestors the humans feared so... We must still feed on the blood of the living. You must understand; this is not our choice."

I nodded, realizing our conversation was now taking a serious turn. He took an old key from the inside pocket of his cloak and nodded towards a small door to his right, a door I'd never been allowed to inquire about before.

"Open it." He said. "Let there no longer be secrets between us."

I took the key anxiously and made my way across the small room towards the door, wary of what might be behind it.

"The child must never know. Do you understand?" He whispered, his voice too weak to raise.

I nodded before turning the key and opening the small, heavy door. Behind it was a tiny room, big enough to fit little more than three people. A woman lay on a bed in the centre, covered in a white cloth. Small plastic tubes ran from her arms, one was releasing a clear liquid into her blood stream; the other was taking the blood from her body and filling up a little bag that hung off the side of the bed.

"The bag becomes full every two days. You must remember to change it…"

I frowned, reaching out to touch the bag of dark red blood.

"Who is she?" I asked, not wanting to remove the white sheet to look.

Viktor paused a few moments before answering me, unsure if he was truly ready to unleash his deepest secrets.

"Emily's mother." He replied, his voice croaking with sadness.

"I thought her mother died?"

He shook his head and sighed.

"Emily's mother was human. When Emily was born we thought she would be human too, I thought she would be able to lead a normal life, but we soon realized she was just like me." He hung his head sadly, as if ashamed. "Emily's mother was sympathetic to our kind, she knew what would happen if the child didn't feed, and Emily wasn't taking to her breast…"

He stopped, taking a few deep breaths before continuing. I stepped out of the small room and locked the door behind me, placing the key into my pocket and taking a seat back beside him.

"Her mother… She sacrificed herself, falling into a never ending sleep so that I could harvest her blood and feed it to the child in secret. Emily has no idea what she is…"

A tear began to form in his eye. He blinked it away quickly and cleared his throat.

"When I am gone, this responsibility will fall on to you. Emily must feed at least once every five days."

I nodded, taking in the information he was giving me and reassuring him I would do right by her.

"How do I give it to her without her knowing?"

He smiled. "Just put it in her food… A little in her lunch, a little in her dinner… Keep her distracted. She mustn't ever know."

I stroked his pale and withering hand, feeling as if I was about to cry myself. I'd grown close to Viktor and hearing him talk about a time he would no longer be around was proving to be rather painful.

"Do not cry." He smiled, cupping my face in his hands. "You must be strong for the child, she depends on you now."

I kissed the palm of his hand and held it against my face, blinking back my tears. I wasn't ready to lose him, he'd become like a brother to me.

"I will… I promise."

Viktor died a few days later. We buried him in the garden, under his favourite apple tree as per his request. Emily can often be found beside his grave, telling him about her day and what she'd been learning. She'd never been to a school. Instead, Viktor had signed her up for online classes which she thoroughly enjoyed. He was afraid allowing her to take part in the outside world would expose their kind and above all else, he just wanted to keep her safe and hidden. I admired him for that.

The day after Viktor's passing I prepared her first blood meal, mixing the dark red liquid into a black pepper sauce and dripping it over steak.

She ate it quickly, commenting on how good it tasted.

"Why aren't you having any?" She asked.

"Oh… I had a big lunch." I smiled, my heart full of nothing but love for my beautiful, half-human child.

About six weeks later, Emily's mother woke up. It was my fault – I wasn't thinking that day. I'd taken Emily out to a museum and had forgotten to top up the anaesthetic before we left. When we got home I sent her upstairs to wash and quickly headed into the basement, locking the door behind me.

She was awake.

Luckily, she'd been asleep for so many years that her muscles had withered and she was unable to move as I topped up the anaesthetic, putting her back to sleep.

As she drifted off, her eyes stared up at me, wild and afraid.

"Help me." She whispered as they finally closed.

# Operation Stargate

My name is Hugh Radcliffe. I served in the Army for 12 years before being recruited for the CIA's Paranormal Espionage Program in 1988. For those that haven't heard about it, the Paranormal Espionage Program, also known as 'Operation Stargate', was an experiment in the 80's and 90's where CIA agents trained members of the forces to travel into what we called 'the ether', something people now commonly refer to as the 'Astral realm'.

I was in my early 30's when I was first introduced to the program. At the time I'd been having vivid nightmares and it was my sergeant who put me in contact with 'S', the leader of the experiment. No one knew his real name, we all went by codes. I was 'Red', due to the fact that my right eye happened to be bloodshot on the day he met me.

I won't go into too much detail about our training or the purpose of the program, but I will tell you what happened on the night of October 31st 1994.

I remember it being a fairly warm day. I arrived at the office around 9am and quickly took my position in one of the 'projection' rooms. The rooms were all painted grey. It was easier to travel without the frequency interference you get with colour, and so we often wore all grey uniforms, even the women painted their nails grey and wore grey eye shadow should they happen to have make-up on.

S had warned me not to travel into the ether on hallows eve. It was an unwritten rule that everyone followed; you don't project on that date, ever. I wasn't superstitious in the slightest and Halloween was nothing more to me than an excuse for kids to dress up and eat candy. So after a couple of years of living by that rule I decided to find out what all the fuss was about.

Before travelling we enter what we called 'decompression', which is basically 15 minutes of 'relaxing time'. Some of us would meditate or listen to calming music, personally I would take a nap – I found it easier to travel if I'd already slept a few minutes beforehand.

"Are you ready?" Chip asked. I wasn't sure why we called him chip, he'd been there much longer than I had, but I assumed it was to do with his love of chips. He was a big man, always eating.

I nodded. "Ready."

"Ok then... Let's begin."

I opened my eyes slightly and let my vision blur as I stared at the blank grey wall. Chip was behind a small window to my left, in a room we called the observation deck. The purpose of this particular journey into the ether was to find a particular Army base and locate a set of documents. Only S knew where they were and what was contained in them.

I started to feel myself leaving my body. I travelled upwards and through the ceiling until I was floating weightlessly above the office building, looking down at the structure below.

"I'm here." I whispered.

"Good." answered Chip. "Travel south-west until..."

"Hang on..." I interrupted, noticing something in the distance I didn't recognize.

"That wasn't there before..."

"What is it?" Chip asked.

I had no idea.

"I'm not sure... I'm going to investigate." I replied, nose-diving towards the mass of glassy black rocks that had appeared beyond the lake that sat just west of our building.

"It's... a building, I think." I reported back, flying around it in a spiral motion. "I don't see any windows, it's more like a cave but it's made from a black, rock, glass kind of material... Am I making sense?"

"I can't see what you're talking about Red. We're looking out the window but there's nothing... Where is it?"

"West, past the lake." I replied. I hate repeating myself...

"Can you get inside?"

On every other mission I've had on this program I've simply flown through a wall or ceiling, when we're in this state we're like ghosts – we can go anywhere, but somehow this building didn't allow for normal procedures.

"I can't get in..." I whispered, confused. "The walls are solid... I don't get it." I tried another area of the building, still nothing worked. I flew down and stood in front of it, looking around for some kind of door.

"How is that possible?" Chip asked.

I had no idea. After a few minutes I noticed a small entrance near the foot of the building and climbed inside.

"I'm in." I whispered.

"What can you see?" Chip asked, he sounded nervous.

"Not much... It looks like a cave." I felt a cold shiver run down my spine as I stepped further into the mysterious building.

"What is this place?" I whispered to myself as I looked around. I couldn't see much, it was full of dark, narrow passages and winding staircases that looked like they were about to collapse any minute.

"Can you see any people? Hear any voices?" Chip asked.

"Nope... empty and silent as far as I can tell..." I answered.

As soon as I said that I heard a noise, a kind of groan.

"Wait... I hear something." I whispered.

"What is it?"

"It's like a wailing...It sounds like someone's in pain..."

I decided to investigate further and headed towards the noise. It sounded like it was coming from one of the narrow passages. I couldn't fly in here, I had to walk as if still in the real world – it was strange, but for some reason I didn't feel concerned.

"What can you see?" Chip asked.

"Nothing – it's too dark to make anything out." I kept walking, squinting in the dark and feeling my way around, trying to find the source of the groaning.

"Hello?" I called. "Who's there?"

The only reply was more groaning. It sounded like a few voices now – not just one.

"I can help you…" I yelled, louder this time. "Tell me where you are!"

The groaning continued. I picked up my pace.

"Your heart rate is increasing." Chip informed me. "What's going on?"

"I'm not sure… It sounds like there's more than one person down here."

"Are you running?" He asked.

"I am…"

"Slow down." His voice was stern. "You're going to give yourself a heart attack, remember your astral body is not used to running."

He was right, I'd never run in the ether before – I'd always flown, but somehow I didn't have that ability in here. I slowed down and began walking again, searching frantically around every corner for the source of the groaning.

"Tell me where you are!" I called. "I can help you!"

Nothing.

"What can you see?" Chips voice was clear and calm.

I looked around. "Nothing… It's getting darker the further in I go. I'm going to keep looking."

Chip paused. "I think you should turn back, I have a bad feeling about this…"

"I'm ok, they're close I know it… I'll head back once I find them and…"

"Red, you need to get out of there."

The fear in his voice brought me to a halt.

"Why, what's wrong?" I asked, trying not to feel anxious.

"Red, the building you're in doesn't exist. There's no building of your description west of the lake. You've entered a different realm and you need to come back, now."

I stood where I was a moment, my interest peaking at his words, a different realm?

"Sir… If I'm in another realm, surely exploring it while I'm here would be in our best interests?"

I could hear his sigh, he wasn't happy but we both knew he couldn't force me to come back, only S had that kind of authority.

"You've got five minutes and I'm bringing you out." He said, irritated I wasn't heeding his warning.

I nodded. "Roger that."

The groaning was getting louder. I knew I was getting close. I started to feel nervous, cold and lost – which after 12 years in the Army was a feeling I wasn't unfamiliar with but it made the hairs on my spine stand on end nonetheless.

At the end of the winding passageway was a small opening with some stairs leading downwards. I took a few steps down, listening to the groaning getting louder still. With each step it got louder and heavier, as if more people were joining in, only it didn't sound like the groans of people, more like wounded animals of some kind.

"What's going on now?" Chip asked calmly.

"I've found a staircase, I'm heading down it."

He didn't respond. I kept walking, noticing what looked like thick metal chains hanging from the walls.

"It looks like some kind of old castle…" I whispered. "Chip… are you there?"

There was no answer. I paused, waiting for a response before continuing. The groaning was almost deafening now, among it I could make out shrieks and howls of agony.

"Sir?" I called out. Still, Chip didn't reply.

'He's probably gone to get S to pull me out' I thought.

"Right then…" I said aloud just in case anyone was still listening. "I'll carry on alone."

I carried on, wondering how far down the staircase went. I couldn't make out the bottom in the dark – I could barely see the next step in front of me. After what felt like a good few minutes, I finally reached the bottom.

"Chip, are you there?" I called.

No answer.

The groaning was right front of me, but I still couldn't see anyone.

"Hello?" I called… nothing.

"Red." S's voice was stern and loud, as if he was shouting right into my ear.

"S?" I asked.

"I told you all missions taking place on this date were to be cancelled, why the hell did you go ahead?"

I froze, not knowing how to respond.

"I… I thought I could do with the practice Sir."

"You are to get out of there this instant. Do you understand me?"

I sighed, not wanting to give up just yet – but also not wanting to be reprimanded for disobeying orders.

"Yes Sir…" I reluctantly replied, turning back to face the staircase.

"Red, do you read me?"

I paused, had he not heard me?

"Yes Sir, returning to base." I replied louder, trying to feel for the stairs in the dark.

"Red, answer me. Return to your body, now!"

I frowned, confused. I had answered him twice now, had he gone deaf?

"I'm trying to find the staircase Sir… I'm sure it was right here…"

"Red, where are you?" Chip called, sounding panicked.

I started to feel anxious, why couldn't they hear me? Had my mouth stopped working? Was I calling out from the spirit world and somehow my body wasn't relaying the message? I had no idea, all I knew was that bad feeling Chip mentioned earlier had suddenly hit home. I was frightened, probably for the first time in years.

"I can't find the stairs Sir…" I called, trying to hide the fear in my voice.

"Red, if you can hear us, you need to return."

"I can hear you!" I yelled, now terrified. I still couldn't find the stairs, I began to run, grasping at the walls trying to find them.

"Red your heart rate is increasing drastically, you need to get out of there now, do you copy?" S was shouting, I could tell he was afraid too. Something wasn't right, something had gone terribly wrong.

"Where the hell is he?" Chip asked.

S sighed, unaware that I could still hear them both.

"He's in hell. That groaning he reported; that's all the other lost souls who have become trapped down there. They're groaning because they've been there so long they've forgotten how to speak."

# Stairs in the Woods

"What is it?" Niro whispered, staring up at the carpeted staircase. "I mean, I know what it is... Why is it here?"

The old man shrugged. "There's a few of them around these parts. They just appear, all different ones, all over. No one knows where they came from."

Aida stepped forward to get a better look.

It would have been normal to see a flight of carpeted stairs had they not been standing in the middle of the woods. Aida and Niro were on a trip with their families to the Grand Canyon and had befriended an old park ranger called Larry who had been guiding their exploration of the surrounding caves and forests for the last few days. It was Saturday, their parents had gone out for dinner and the girls and Larry were on their way back to their tents when they came across the stairs.

"How long has this one been here?" Aida asked, noticing the clean and new looking carpet and un-spoiled hand rails.

Larry shrugged for the second time. "I haven't seen this one before, but it looks fairly new."

"What happens if you go up?" Niro asked nervously, eyeing the drop between the final step and the ground.

"Never go up." Larry warned, catching sight of Aida as she edged towards the staircase.

"Why?" Aida asked, not looking back.

"You just don't touch them. It's said that anyone who does... They go missing. And I don't want that on my conscience you hear? Let's go."

He turned and began continuing the walk back to their tents, ushering the girls to follow him. Niro nodded and scurried along quickly beside him.

Aida sighed. "Ok…" She muttered, following behind.

"Good. Whenever you see things like that you just leave them well alone. Good folk got no business messin' with things like that."

Niro looked up at him. "Why?" She asked.

He sighed. "Because whatever brought them here is…" He froze, noticing the sound of Aida's footsteps as they grew faster and further away. "Aida!" He yelled, spinning around.

"Aida!" Niro shouted, running after her friend.

"No." Larry stepped forwards and grabbed her, holding Niro back from the stairs.

Aida kept running. She didn't glance back to Niro and the old man as she reached the bottom of the mysterious staircase, laughing.

She looked up and smiled.

'It's just stairs.' She thought, before taking the first step.

"No!" Niro shouted.

Larry squeezed her arm.

"One…" Aida whispered, smiling as she stood on the bottom step. The carpet felt strangely familiar but she didn't pay it much thought.

She giggled as she took the second, then the third.

"What is she doing?" Larry wondered out loud, thinking of all the people reported missing who at one point on their travels, had come across a mysterious staircase in the woods.

Aida continued on up the stairs, looking around at the trees and sky as she ascended higher. Finally she reached the top step; the thirteenth step.

She stood and looked around for a moment, giggling to herself at the view and silliness of it all. Here she was, in the woods by the Grand Canyon, at the top of a random carpeted staircase they found with an old park ranger they had met only a few days ago. She laughed at the odd situation she found herself in, waving at Niro and Larry from the top of the stairs.

"See… She's ok." Niro smiled.

Larry sighed as Niro ran forwards to greet Aida. "For now..." He muttered under his breath.

Aida descended the stairs quickly and ran to Niro laughing. "See! They're just stairs." She smiled.

Niro hugged her friend before playfully punching her in the arm.

"Don't do that shit!" She laughed as they headed back to their tents.


A few weeks later Aida and Niro were home and settling back in to their normal routines. The girls only lived a few minutes away from each other and so spent most weekends having sleepovers and riding their bikes up and down the quiet road. On this occasion, they had been to the Harlequin center to buy outfits for Aida's upcoming birthday party and were now getting ready for bed.

Aida yawned as she pulled on a large baggy t-shirt and tracksuit bottoms before climbing into the bed next to Niro. Niro had on a pair of shorts and one of Aida's old t-shirts and was already curled up under the duvet with her eyes closed as Aida snuggled down and turned off the light.

It was about three minutes before Aida whispered "Are you awake?"

Niro giggled and whispered back. "Yes."

The light flicked back on and Aida sat up. "I can't sleep... You want to watch a film?"

Niro smiled and rolled over, stretching before sitting up and facing her friend. "Ok." She replied. "But no horrors."

Aida laughed and stood up. "Ok, you pick a film and I'll get snacks."

Niro nodded and crawled to the foot of the bed, scanning the DVD collection whilst Aida headed downstairs. She decided on a comedy and placed the DVD carefully in the player before getting back into bed with the remote to wait for Aida.

Aida was in the kitchen, raiding her parent's pantry for as many snacks as she could find. She filled a bowl with popcorn, placed some crisps, chocolates, biscuits and bottles of juice on a tray and headed back into the hall. As she walked towards the stair case she felt a cold shiver run up her spine, as if something was watching her. She looked around nervously in the dark. Her parents were both in bed...

As she reached the bottom of the stairs she looked up, remembering the stairs in the woods from a few weeks before and realizing they looked almost identical to her own. She hadn't realised it at the time – without the wallpaper and hanging photographs it was hard to recognize them – but she was sure of it, they were the same stairs.

She froze.

'They're just stairs...' She thought to herself as she lifted her foot, ready to take the first step.

Niro had turned on the DVD by now and was fast forwarding through the adverts when she heard a crash from the stairs. She paused the DVD and glanced over to the bedroom door, giggling at the thought of Aida having tripped and dropped everything.

"Are you ok?" She called.

There was no answer. She climbed out of bed and walked over to the doorway, turning on the hall light and glancing down the stairs. No one was there. Just a tray at the bottom of the stairs with an overturned bowl of popcorn and other snacks...

Niro looked over to the bathroom, wondering if Aida had been seriously hurt and gone in there to nurse a broken wrist or something. The door was open and the light was off so she knew it wasn't likely, but she checked anyway.

Nothing.

She began walking down the stairs calling for her friend. All the lights were off and Aida was nowhere to be seen.

"Aida?!" Niro shouted, becoming more and more frantic. Aida's parents appeared at the top of the stairs.

"What's going on?" Her mother called noticing the mess.

"I can't find Aida..."

"What do you mean?" Asked her father.

Niro looked up, unsure of what to do or say...

"She's just...gone."

Somewhere in the vast and untamed land that surrounded the Grand Canyon was a woods, and in that woods was a carpeted staircase.

At the top of that carpeted staircase sat a girl, who had just suddenly appeared from nowhere.

"Hello?" She called out into the dark.

# The Vampire of Highgate

"They say if you walk through the cemetery of Highgate at night you'll see him. He is remarkably well kept for a man living in a graveyard, with his long black cloak and top hat you'd think he was some kind of prince. I guess that's how he lures his victims; they assume he's rich and follow him. Either that or he just hypnotizes them. I stay away from that part of town."

Daniel listened as Katie tossed her tennis ball into the air, catching it and throwing it again as she spoke.

"He's not real though, is he?" He asked.

She stopped walking and glared at him as if offended by the question. "Of course he is." She snapped. "Why would he not be real?"

Daniel shrugged. "Well, you're talking about a vampire here – it's not like there's a lot of proof of their existence…"

"You're an idiot." Katie replied, rolling her eyes and continuing her walk. Daniel scrambled to catch up as she marched off down the road.

"If you don't think he's real, go spend a night in the graveyard. I dare you."

He laughed. "I'm not going to spend a night in a graveyard I'll get hypothermia or something…"

"You scared?" Katie cut him off, raising an eyebrow at his excuse for not following through on his dare.

"Of a mythological creature? I'm ok. I'm more worried about the hobo's to be quite honest."

Katie laughed as they entered a small coffee shop and sat down, both ordering hot chocolates and continuing their conversation about the Highgate vampire.

"There was this old woman who lived down the road from me, she used to go and visit her husband in the graveyard in the evenings to say goodnight and tell him about her day. Well, one day she just never came back. They found her body tucked behind some bushes a few days later – she looked like she'd been torn apart by an animal..."

"And you think it was the vampire?" Daniel interrupted.

Katie frowned. "What else could it be? Her body was drained of blood."

"Was it? Or did she just trip and bleed a bit from her injuries and you exaggerated the rest in your head?"

Katie scowled and sipped on her hot chocolate, ignoring Daniel's smug responses.

"Like I said; if you want to prove me wrong – spend a night there." Katie smiled.

Daniel rolled his eyes. "I'll go at midnight for an hour or two but I'm not spending the night there. I have things to do tomorrow."

Katie laughed and opened her mouth to reply but was distracted by the tall red haired woman who had suddenly appeared at the end of their table. Daniel looked up, noticing her also and opening his mouth to let her know they had already been served, but she spoke before he could.

"If you want to see the vampire you have to go at 3am."

The pair froze for a moment before Katie asked. "Why 3am? Witching hour?"

The strange woman shrugged and replied. "Pubs all close at 2am. I guess it gives everyone an hour to get home before he comes out. Less chance of being seen."

Daniel frowned. "But doesn't he eat people?"

The woman laughed. "Rarely. He likes a sausage casserole most nights."

Katie wasn't impressed and wrinkled her nose in distaste for the woman's rude interruption before asking; "And how do you know so much about it?"

The woman shrugged. "I take interest in these kinds of things."

Daniel nodded nervously before looking back to Katie, not knowing what to say or how to respond to the red haired stranger.

"So... You know where to find him?" Katie asked.

The woman nodded. "Meet me at the entrance to the cemetery at 2:45 tonight and I'll take you straight to him." She smiled before adding, "Oh – My name is Victoria, it's nice to meet you both."

"I'm Dan, that's Kate. See you later..." Daniel nodded politely as she left before turning to Katie and whispering; "We're not really going to go, are we?"

Katie smiled. "Oh yes we are. I'll pick you up at 2:30. Make sure you're awake! And bring your camera."

Daniel laughed and shook his head. "I hate you." He muttered as he finished his drink.


A few hours later and Dan was at home with his parents, discussing the events he had planned for later that night.

"Oh I see, like ghost hunting but for vampires?" His mother asked as she ate her dinner.

"Will you be fashioning your own wooden stake or do they sell them online these days?" His father chuckled.

Daniel shook his head and laughed, embarrassed by the situation. "I have no idea what she's got planned but I'm drawing the line at garlic necklaces."

His mother laughed. "Oh but you'd look so handsome in one!" She smiled, pinching his cheek.

Neither of his parents were worried, they'd lived in Highgate for some time and had heard all the vampire stories there were. The little old lady who slipped, the drunk homeless man who got hypothermia, the little red haired girl who got bitten and 'turned' – they knew it was all just stories people made up to scare the kids.

Daniel went to sleep about 9pm and set him alarm for 2am. He wanted to eat before his midnight adventure with Katie and the mysterious girl they'd met in the coffee shop.

It didn't take him long to drift off and within the hour he was in a deep sleep, dreaming about the night ahead.

At 2am his alarm woke him with a high pitched ring. Daniel groaned and hit the snooze button before rolling over to catch a few more minutes sleep, but he couldn't. Rolling his eyes he climbed out of bed, stretched and headed into the bathroom for a shower.

When he returned to his bedroom he noticed a text message from Katie; "You better be up and getting ready." It said. Daniel chuckled and threw his phone down on the bed, pulling on a clean shirt, boxers and jeans and heading downstairs to grab a quick bite to eat.

By 2:28am Daniel was waiting outside his front gate for Katie, watching his breath form clouds in the cold autumn air. She arrived a few minutes later.

"How's it going?" She asked as she approached him, leaning in for a hug.

"Good." He whispered back, not wanting to wake any neighbours. "I brought my camera."

Katie smiled at the old canon camera that hung around his neck. It was the one his mother used to take all their sports day pictures on when they were kids, pictures which she now had hanging around the mirror in her bedroom.

They began their walk to the cemetery, discussing what they thought the night ahead would hold for them both.

"What if there really is a vampire?" Katie wondered out loud.

"There isn't. It's probably just some eccentric old drunk..."

"For God's sake Dan I'm just saying *imagine* if there is. What would you do?"

Dan thought about it for a minute.

"I'd take a picture of it." He said finally. "If it's a real vampire it won't show up in pictures because camera's use mirrors, right?"

Katie shrugged. "I guess."

"Right then. So if anyone's at the cemetery, I'll take a picture of them and if they show up in the photo – that settles it."

Katie sighed and nodded. "But what if it's an evolved vampire and it can show up in pictures now. They say they don't have reflections because of something to do with the silver in the mirror, but mirrors aren't always made with silver nowadays, right?"

"Like they're allergic to silver?" Dan asked, wrinkling his nose at Katie's theory.

"I think so. That's why you can kill them with a silver bullet."

Dan rolled his eyes dramatically. "So, we're looking for a vampire that carries antihistamines. Awesome."

They arrived at the cemetery gates around 2:50am and waited for Victoria. The gates were padlocked shut and too high to climb. Katie wondered if Victoria knew of another way in.

As if reading her mind, Victoria appeared from the shadows and lit a cigarette.

"I didn't think you would come." She smiled, turning and beckoning them both to follow her.

Katie and Dan fell silent as they followed the red haired woman into some bushes, through a broken fence and into the large cemetery, emerging from behind the church itself.

"Wow..." Katie giggled as they entered the graveyard. "How did you even know that was there?"

Victoria smiled and shrugged her shoulder.

"I have my ways. Come." She gestured to a small corner of the graveyard and crouched down behind a large headstone, nodding at Katie and Dan to do the same. They followed her instruction and took their places beside her, watching and waiting for something to happen.

"What are we looking for?" Dan whispered after a few moments.

"The vampire, obviously." Katie replied, rolling her eyes.

"The bats." Victoria corrected, looking up into the sky at the small group of bats that were circling overhead.

"Jesus Christ..." Dan mumbled, fiddling around for his camera.

Victoria held out her hand to stop him. "Not yet." She whispered. "The noise..."

Dan nodded and put it down, not taking his eyes off the sky, or more specifically – the bats.

"What are they doing?" Katie asked.

Victoria smiled and looked over to another large headstone on the opposite side of the church garden. It was half hidden by trees and rose bushes but you could just make out the large black angel on top of it.

"They're waking him up." She smiled.

The bats began to descend, swooping low into the graveyard before flying up again to the roof of the church. The angel on top of the large headstone began to move.

"Can you see him? Over there..." Victoria pointed him out to Dan and Katie as he stepped down onto the grass and took a deep breath. What they had originally thought were wings of an angel became a long black cloak. His hair was long and black and his features sharp and unnaturally pointed.

"No way." Katie gasped, clasping her hand to her mouth to muffle the sound of her voice, not wanting to disturb the creature.

"That can't be for real..." Dan whispered. "Have you set this up?" He turned to Victoria accusingly.

Victoria raised her eyebrow and nodded towards his camera. "Take your picture." She whispered.

Dan picked up his camera and aimed it at the creature, taking a deep breath before taking the photo. He could feel himself shaking with fear as he focused the lens...

Click.

The shutter sound was louder with the silence of their surroundings. Dan froze, too scared to move.

Slowly he took the camera away from his face and reviewed the image. It was an empty graveyard.

"No..." Dan shook his head in disbelief, raising the camera to his face to take another picture.

Click.

"No..."

Click.

"No…"

Click.

"Dan!" Katie tore the camera away from him and threw her hand over his mouth, muffling his cries.

The vampire looked up suddenly, sniffing the air.

"You've done it now." Victoria sighed, shaking her head.

"What the fuck is that?" Katie whispered through tears.

"That's your vampire." Victoria smiled, standing up and pointing over to the creature that was now staring right at them. "Don't you want to take some pictures?"

Foolishly, Dan picked up his camera as the vampire turned and began making its way slowly towards them. Shaking with nerves he took a picture and quickly reviewed it, showing it to Katie. Neither Victoria, nor the creature could be seen in the photo. The whole area was in frame, how could they have just disappeared?

Suddenly, the truth dawned on them both.

"Run." He whispered.


Two days later Dan and Katie's bodies were found dumped behind the church bin. Both had been drained of blood. I think it's safe to say Dan's parents now believe in the Highgate vampire.

And if you're wondering how I know exactly what happened to them – well, I'll give you a clue.

My hair is red, and I take interest in these things…

# Project Black Box

"I lost it…" Came a sad and timid voice from the doorway. Eli looked up from the book he was just getting in to and sighed.

"I knew it wouldn't take long. Where did you lose it?"

Mia stayed silent. She obviously wasn't keen on being very precise about her location – which led Eli to believe she'd been playing where she shouldn't have been. He sighed again and put his book on the table beside him, shaking his head as he stood.

"Come on then, let's go get it."

"Are you mad at me?" Mia asked, her blue eyes glistening with the beginning of tears.

Eli chuckled gently and placed a hand on her shoulder, turning her around and leading her towards the front door.

"Why would I be mad?"

Mia shrugged sadly. "Because you only just made it for me and I lost it already… I didn't mean to."

He squeezed her shoulder reassuringly. "Of course you didn't, accidents happen, don't worry about it."

They left the house quickly, heading towards the fields on the other side of town. Mia stayed quiet as they walked, she hated disappointing her brother and the last thing he'd said to her before she went out to play was "Don't lose it." She felt guilty, ashamed almost.

"Hey, chin up it's no big deal." Eli smiled, noticing her glum expression. Mia smiled weakly back at him, thankful that he was being understanding rather than angry – she knew it had taken him weeks to make. They crossed the fields and headed into the woods.

"Damn, how far did you go?" Eli asked. Mia stayed quiet. The number one rule had always been not to go too far from the house and she felt awful for disobeying it.

"It's just over there..." She pointed to a bridge in the distance.

"By the bridge?" Eli asked.

"No..." Mia answered sadly. "Just beyond that..."

Eli stared at her for a moment, he'd never even gone that far before, what on earth was she doing this far out? Mia didn't say anything else. Eli didn't either, not until they got to the bridge anyway.

"So, where is it?"

"This way." Mia pointed ahead, carrying on walking deeper into the woods.

"Mia, what the hell were you doing this far away from the house?"

Mia shrugged, she didn't know what to say. She looked up at him sadly, still wondering if he was secretly mad at her. Eli rolled his eyes.

"Don't worry about it – just don't do it again ok?"

Mia nodded. They continued to walk for another five minutes or so before finally stopping at a tall brick wall that went on for as far as they could see. Eli noticed a small bundle of white string entangled over the bark of a fallen tree.

"Over there?" He asked.

Mia shook her head. "That's just the string... The kite went over the wall." She answered quietly. She wasn't sure how they would ever get it back.

Eli frowned, now he was starting to get annoyed.

"It went over the wall." He repeated. "Great. And how do you think I'm supposed to get it back?"

Mia said nothing. She wasn't quite sure what she thought Eli would be able to do – the wall was over ten feet high, but he was her big brother, her hero – he had an answer for everything. Surely he'd find a way? Eli sighed, looking around for something to use as a step ladder. He noticed the fallen tree the string was tangled up on.

"Here..." He said. "Help me move this."

Mia nodded, helping him drag the small broken tree to the foot of the wall. They leant it up against it, digging it into the ground and fixing it in place against the wall, its branches just reaching the top. Mia smiled; she knew he'd think of something.

"Wait here." Eli said as he began climbing the trunk of the small tree. Mia stood at the bottom, watching him and wondering how he was going to get down the other side. When he reached the top he sat on the wall catching his breath, his legs either side.

"Can you see it?" Mia asked. Eli shook his head.

"I can see the string, just not where it goes..." He replied.

"Oh." Mia sighed sadly.

"Hold up..." Eli shouted as he shuffled onto his stomach and dropped over the other side. Mia's eyes widened as she heard the thud of her brothers landing.

"Are you ok?" She shouted.

"Eli?"

Nothing.

Mia frowned, why wasn't he answering? She waited a few moments.

"Eli?" She called again, her voice slightly more worried this time. Still, no reply came.

She glanced up at the wall, she wasn't good with heights, even just looking at it made her feel queasy.

"Eli are you ok?"

Still nothing.

Mia suddenly became all too aware of how alone she was, how quiet it was. How she hadn't seen another person the entire day. She felt nervous.

"Eli?" She called desperately one last time, what if he'd hurt himself? She couldn't risk it. She took a deep breath and began to climb the tree.

"What are you doing?" Came a rough voice from behind her. Mia turned around quickly, almost losing her balance. She looked up to see a tall man in jeans and a white polo shirt, he held out his hand and smiled, offering to help her down. Mia looked back nervously towards the wall, willing her brother to climb back over and join her. She'd never seen this man before...

"Who are you?" Mia asked. Her voice was shaky and fragile. The man smiled again and gestured for her to take his hand and climb down. She stayed where she was, waiting for him to answer.

"My name is Dr Black. I am the creator of this program." He smiled again, proudly. Mia looked around, unsure of what he meant.

"What program?" She asked.

Dr Black gestured again for her to climb down and join him, this time she did as she was told, glancing back to the wall to check for her brother. He still hadn't returned, or even called out for that matter. She wondered if he was hurt...

"My brother..." She began.

"Don't worry about him." Dr Black interrupted. "He's just a simulation, he'll be back in the morning."

Mia frowned, confused at his response. Dr Black chuckled.

"Come. Walk with me." He said. "I'll tell you all about it."

Mia nodded and climbed down gingerly, being careful about where she placed her bare feet. She stood down next to him, looking up into his dark eyes. She felt like she'd seen him before... in a dream maybe.

"Good girl." He smiled. His smile made her feel uneasy, it was more of a smirk – she didn't like it at all. Mia looked back over her shoulder, wishing her brother would come back and tell this Dr Black to go away. Alas, nothing happened. She looked back to the stranger, who was holding out his arm, nodding for her to take it. She did, reluctantly.

"Tell me," Dr Black started, "What is your earliest memory?"

Mia was taken aback by the question, she'd never really thought about her memories before, let alone her earliest one.

"My brother made me a kite..." She began, stopping when she realized that had only happened earlier that day. She tried to think of another one, one from her childhood maybe. She couldn't.

"I don't know..." She answered sadly.

Dr Black smiled again. "Ah, in that case our program is working exactly as it should." He looked down at her, eager to explain.

"Everything you see here on this side of the wall is a simulation. Every day you do the same thing you did the day before without realizing, because every night we wipe your memory..."

Mia stopped walking and pulled her arm away from him, she stared up at him in disbelief, what did he mean? She had no idea what he was talking about, or why he would say those things.

"I know, quite the shock isn't it?" He chuckled. "Your parents were part of a very important scientific experiment. We called it project black box – which is where I got the name Dr Black. It's called black box because for us, your world is simply a large black box. Everything inside the black box is just a simulation to keep you busy while we work out how to deal with your kind."

"My kind?" Mia asked, even more confused than ever.

"Yes. You are part of a group of people we call the Expansion. The expansion was a neurological development, in part; an experiment to see if we could enhance the capabilities of the average human. We did this by enlarging the parts of the brain used for decoding universal energy into what we've come to know as consciousness. After successfully achieving this with a small group of four humans, two males and two female; we created the breeding program, which is where you came from." He smiled, placing his hand on Mia's back and directing her across the bridge she had walked over earlier with her brother.

"For the first ten years of your life you were placed with an ex-NASA scientist; Marie Cardell. She was your handler for a while, keeping an eye on how you developed and reporting back to us with any significant changes in your behavior or awareness. That is until you killed her."

Mia looked up in shock, her mouth hanging open at the prospect of her being a murderer. Could it be true? She couldn't remember. She couldn't remember anything...

"I know, sad isn't it, someone as young as yourself could do such a thing. You didn't realize what you had done, it wasn't purposeful. You weren't made aware of your capabilities or the extent of your powers – partly because we didn't know ourselves and partly because we wanted to see if and how you would discover them on your own. After the murder, you ran. It took us three years to track you down and bring you here."

Mia felt a single tear make its way down her face, how could she be a murderer? She'd never even trod on a bug before, it just wasn't in her nature...

"So this is a prison?" She asked, her voice quivering with confusion and fear.

"Not quite, more like a holding facility until we figure out what to do with you. You see, the leaders of the true world don't have long left before we leave the planet. Most of the experiments will be coming with us so we can utilize their abilities and use them for the progression of the new world, but a lot will be staying behind. The ones that stay behind will have to be killed off, we don't want them coming after us seeking revenge now do we?" He chuckled again. Mia felt sick.

"So you're going to kill me?" She asked.

Dr Black frowned, as if her question were ludicrous.

"My dear, if we could kill you we'd of done it already. The sad fact of the matter is we haven't figured out how to do it yet, which is why we have you here – so we can keep an eye on you, study you – until we figure out how to do it." He seemed proud of the idea, as if it brought him the greatest joy on earth.

"Why are you telling me this?" Mia asked, a sudden surge of anger coursing through her body.

Dr Black shrugged. "You'll forget we even had this conversation in a few hours, plus – it'll be interesting to see how you react." He continued guiding her home, his hand pressed firmly on her back. She shrugged him off as she walked, a deep loathing growing in the pit of her stomach.

"How long have I been here?" She asked, her voice louder than before, more demanding and confident.

Dr Black continued walking, picking up his pace. Mia struggled to keep up with him.

"Eight years. Your siblings are being held in similar units, some of them have never known anything else. It's an interesting facility we have here, if you behave yourself I might even show you around one day."

Mia's lips pursed shut and her eyes darted around nervously as she struggled to process the information she'd just taken in, how could it be true?

They crossed the fields and entered the small empty village, walking quickly to the house on the other side. Mia stopped as they reached the door.

"What's the problem?" Dr Black asked, as if nothing in the world could be wrong. Mia stared at him in utter disbelief, she was lost for words.

"Come on, I'm a busy man – inside please."

Mia did as she was told, not knowing what else she could do.

"What's beyond the wall?" She asked nervously as she stepped past him and entered through the front door of her house.

Dr Black smiled. "Nothing, it's just an illusion – part of the simulation to make the experience more real. What did you see when you looked?"

Mia thought for a moment. "Fields, mostly..." She answered. "What would have happened if I jumped over it?"

Dr Black chuckled before closing the door behind them and answering.

"You'd have probably broken your legs for starters. The wall is about 18 feet high on our side, ten feet on yours. Alarms would have sounded and you'd have been gassed, hospitalized and then put back in once you were fixed. It's happened before."

Mia's eyes widened. "To me?" She asked. Dr Black nodded.

"The kite went over the wall for the first time about 7 months ago, you broke your right ankle and wrist, it was a wonder that's all you did really. Go ahead, check the scars if you don't believe me."

Mia pulled up the sleeve of her shirt and inspected her wrist, sure enough; three small scars were there, barely noticeable. She was rendered speechless once again. Dr Black smiled.

"Lay down, take a nap. When you wake up your brother will be here and everything will be back to normal." He gestured towards the sofa. Mia shook her head.

"Please don't, I don't want to forget…"

Dr Black shook his head. "I know, you say that every time, but it's for your own good. We don't want you planning another escape now do we?"

Mia's eyes welled up with tears as she willed herself not to cry. She needed to think, to focus and find some way – any way to help herself remember.

"Come on now, get comfortable." He ushered her towards the sofa and sat her down, tucking a blanket around her like a father. Mia stared into space, not knowing how to react. She lay down with her head on the arm of the sofa.

"Good girl." He grinned, standing up and heading towards the front door. "Now, close your eyes and go to sleep. Everything will be fine, don't stress yourself." He nodded once and left as quickly as he'd appeared by the tree. Mia sat up and looked out the window, he was gone. Completely gone. Where did he go? She could feel her heart beating a thousand times an hour, her palms and forehead were clammy with sweat – what was this place? She stood up and went to the window. That's why the village was so empty – it wasn't real… She ran upstairs to her bedroom and found a bunch of felt tip markers. As quickly as she could she ran around the house and wrote on all the walls; 'It's not real', 'It's not real', 'It's not real'… She was frantic, panicking. Suddenly she heard a hiss, as if someone had opened a tap in the next room. She looked out of her window. Small gas clouds began rising, seeping out from the roads and lampposts. Nearly everything in sight was letting out a wispy grey smoke. The light fittings above her began hissing, gas was coming from them too… Her eyes widened in horror as she dropped to the floor, holding her hands over her mouth in an attempt to keep herself from breathing it in. She looked at the felt tips and grabbed one, quickly writing on her own hand, 'Go to wall. 18 feet drop. Get out, don't let them gas you' as the world grew darker and her eyes began to close...

Mia woke up to the sound of a tap running in the bathroom. She rubbed her eyes and sat up slowly, looking around for her brother.

"Eli?" She called. He came in a moment later, a bucket of warm soapy water in one hand and a large sponge in the other.

"Awake are we? I take it you wore yourself out with all the vandalism you got up to last night?" He replied sarcastically. Mia frowned, unsure of what he meant. He nodded towards the far wall. A faded red smudge remained and coloured felt tip pens littered the floor around her. She raised her hand to her head.

"I don't remember doing that..." She mumbled groggily.

Eli sighed. "It's fine, I'll clean up, you go get yourself some breakfast." He walked over to the wall and began scrubbing at it. Mia nodded, standing up and walking into the kitchen, her eyes glancing at all the coloured marks on the walls as she walked past them. What did they say? What would compel her to vandalize her own home? She got herself breakfast and tried to forget about it. She stared out into the garden as she ate her cereal, it was a nice day, maybe she'd go for a walk later.

"So, now that's all cleared up – I've got a surprise for you." Eli declared as he entered the room. Mia looked up from the table and smiled, she knew he'd been making her a kite for the last few weeks and couldn't wait to see it.

"Is it finished?" She asked excitedly. Eli nodded, opening a small cupboard next to the back door and taking out a package. He'd wrapped it and everything. Mia squealed as she tore open the paper, grinning at the colours that met her eyes.

"Oh Eli it's wonderful!" She smiled, throwing her arms around his neck for a hug. Eli smiled, glad that he could make her happy.

"Why don't you take it into the fields and try it out?" He suggested.

Mia's grin grew wider and she hopped up and down with excitement.

"Ok! I'll be back in a bit!" She ran out of the room to put her shoes on without even finishing her breakfast.

"Hold up..." Eli called after her, following her out into the hallway.

"Here, take a key. I might be out by the time you get back."

Mia nodded, holding out her hand for the key Eli was fishing out of the drawer. He frowned as his eyes caught the state of her hand.

"What's that?" He asked, taking hold of it in his.

"18 feet drop, get out, don't let them gas you? What on Earth is that about?"

Mia looked down at her hand in confusion, she didn't remember writing that...

"I don't know..." She answered.

"Come on, wash your hands and then you can go."

Mia nodded, putting her new kite on the sofa and heading upstairs to the bathroom. She began washing the ink from her hand, still wandering what it could mean? 18 feet drop... What is? Get out... Why? Don't let them gas you... Who's gassing who, and what for? Unable to make sense of the strange message, she shrugged it off and headed back downstairs, taking the key and leaving through the front door. She couldn't tell if the sick feeling in her stomach was due to the strange happenings of this morning or was simply excitement to try out her new kite. She couldn't get those questions out of her mind...

"Don't lose it!" Eli called as she closed the door behind her.

"I won't..."

# Mama Llarona

They call her the weeping woman, or the woman in white. An old wives tale parents tell to get their children to behave, or so we like to believe that's all it is...

The story goes that La Llarona was a beautiful woman in the mid 1800's, a proud Mexican woman with two children. She was betrothed to a man of status and great wealth and was looking forward to her future with him. One evening, La Llarona discovered her man had been unfaithful and was planning to leave her for a younger, more attractive woman. In the heat of a manic rage, La Llarona left her home with her two children and took them to a nearby river, in which she drowned them both. Upon realizing what she had done, she went home and slit her own throat in what would have been her future marital bed.

They say that when she got to heaven she was denied entry because she didn't have the souls of her children with her, so she returned to Earth in search for them. To this day she wanders the riverbank searching for her lost children, growing angry and attacking those who cross her path. Recorded sightings are now reaching the thousands and anyone unlucky enough to have met her for a second time is sure to meet a watery grave.

Well.

It turns out she actually had three children. The oldest child she had in secret when she was 14. The child had been adopted by La Llarona's Aunt Ivanna. Nobody really mentioned him in the La Llarona stories, I don't think people even knew he existed. When he was 27 he married and had 4 children, one of which was my father's abuela; Mama Llarona – named after her infamous ancestor for reasons I will never quite understand.

I don't really remember mama Llarona, she died when I was little, but I remember her telling the story of her father's mother, who's restless spirit would come and get us should we misbehave. We lived in California, a place known for La Llarona sightings almost as much as New Mexico, and when the kids in my class found out about my family tree I became an instant celebrity among the 'weird kids', the ones who liked all that ghost hunting stuff. I was often asked questions about her and found myself telling the same stories over and over again at break times to different groups of students and teachers who found great interest in my family's history. It soon died down though, and as I grew up people just stopped asking about it. I guess they'd heard it all before.

I'm 25 now, and in my third year at University. I'm studying psychology and my friends are doing media, art, music, astrophysics etc. So I only see them once or twice a week. Last Saturday the boys all came round mine for some drinks. It turned out they also had a proposition for me.

"We've got to make a short film for the course, so basically..." Nicolas began. He was the media student.

I smiled, knowing exactly where this was going.

"You want to make a film about La Llarona." I finished his sentence for him.

He laughed awkwardly. "A documentary... Would that be ok?"

I nodded. "Sure, I don't mind."

Dorian smiled. "Cool. I'm going to be doing all the sound for it." He said, clearly excited for the project. He's the art and music major.

"Awesome." I grinned, looking at Chan and waiting to see if he was going to be involved as well.

"I'll tag along." He nodded, taking a sip of his beer. "Sounds interesting."

And just like that we were going to make a documentary about the ghost of my dead relative. We met again the following Friday to film the first couple of scenes. We started off at mine, with me telling the famous story of La Llarona. After that we called my father and heard it from him. Then we walked the streets talking to locals and asking them for their own versions of the well-known tale. By the end of the day we had filmed the first part of Nicolas's documentary. He was pretty excited about it, apparently everyone else in his class was doing fashion films and music videos – he was the only one doing a documentary on the supernatural, meaning his work in particular was sure to stand out against the rest.

The following day we met again to continue our filming. This time we decided to take a train down to the river where La Llorona was said to have drowned her children. We woke up early and arrived on location by about 10am.

"It just feels creepy!" Dorian exclaimed as we set down our bags by the river bank.

"You're not wrong there..." Nicolas agreed, looking around at the low hanging trees and the moss covered rocks.

Chan took some pictures on his phone as Nicolas set up his tripod. It was strange to be there, I'd never visited this river before, even though its name had been mentioned in my house about a thousand times. I looked into the murky waters... Was this the spot my ancestor had murdered her children, or was it further down? Would I get a cold shiver or something when we found it or would I just never know? I wasn't sure how to process the situation we were in.

"You ready?" Nicolas called out to me. I hadn't realized I'd wandered off...

I turned around and walked back towards my friends.

Dorian handed me a bottle of water as he set up the boom mic. "Stay hydrated." He said with a wink. I laughed and slipped the bottle into the back pocket of my baggy jeans. "Ready when you are." He nodded at Nicolas, positioning the boom mic above my head.

"Ok, rolling..." Nicolas called. Chan turned around to watch us, losing interest in his new photography habit now some real action was afoot. "And, ACTION!"

I hid my chuckles at Nicolas's enthusiasm as he began introducing the scene.

"So, this is the first time you've ever been here?" He asked, turning the attention on me as we began walking up and down the river bank.

"Yep. First time." I answered.

"How does it feel as a descendant of La Llarona to be walking on the river where she drowned her children?"

I shivered at the thought of even stepping foot into those cold, murky waters, I can't imagine how it would feel drowning in them.

"It's pretty chilling." I replied. "I guess it's weird knowing someone I'm related to could do that…"

We filmed until the battery ran out on Nicolas's camera, which altogether was probably about two hours' worth of footage – much more than he needed. At around 2:30pm we began the journey home, stopping for lunch on the way.

I didn't hear much else about it for a week or so.

Then I got a call.

"You need to come to Nicolas's… There's something we gotta' show you…" Dorian said quietly over the phone.

"Can it wait?" I asked, glancing over to the chill-con-carne I was just about to start heating up in the microwave.

"I think you should come now."

I sighed. "Ok cool. I'm on my way."

I put my dinner back in the fridge and caught an Uber over to Nicolas's, wondering what all the fuss was about. Dorian sounded pretty uneasy on the phone…

"Hey…" Chan smiled nervously as he opened the door.

"How's it going?"

I raised an eyebrow and stepped inside.

"Good… how's things with you?"

He nodded and gulped, as if there was something troubling him that he couldn't tell me.

We walked into the front room and met the other two, who were sitting at Nicolas's laptop.

"Hey." Dorian nodded as I came through.

I smiled and nodded in return. "You alright?"

He stood up and offered me the seat next to Nicolas so I could get a better look at whatever it was they needed to show me.

"What is it?" I asked, sitting down and facing the laptop.

"Just watch..." Nicolas sighed, tilting the laptop towards me so I had the better view.

He pressed play.

I watched the screen as it played the footage the boys and I had filmed the week before. Rolling my eyes at the way the wind was blowing my hair. I hadn't realised how badly I needed a haircut...

"Did you see her?" Chan asked after a minute.

"See who?" I asked. No one had told me to watch out for anything...

Nicolas rewound the video a few seconds and hit play.

"Look here." He said, pointing to the top left hand corner of the screen at an old willow tree.

I watched, waiting for something to happen...

And then it did.

I froze. Not knowing where to look or what to say... There she was, gliding across the river, levitating right above it as her long dark hair floated behind her.

"No one was there..." Was all I could say.

"We were alone... Who is that?"

"I think it's your great granny dude." Dorian murmured, his eyes just as wide and fearful as the rest of us.

Nicolas rewound it for me to watch again, this time slowing it down.

In the video you can see me walking alongside the river bank, talking about how it feels to be related to a murderer. Just as I mention her name, a woman in a long white dress appears further down the river, floating just above it and looking right at us. Specifically, me.

"What do you think she's saying?" I ask, pointing at her moving lips.

Chan leans forward and studies her lips for the second before she disappears into thin air.

"I'm not sure…" He replied. "Can we zoom in?"

"Sure, one sec." Nicolas nodded and fiddled with the laptop for a moment before turning it back around to face us and playing the footage again. This time he'd zoomed in to her mouth.

My eyes widened, instantly recognizing the movement of her lips. It was something my mother said to me almost every day…

"What is it?" Nicolas asked.

"Mijo…" I answered. "She thinks I'm her kid…"

The footage played for another few moments as we sat there in silence, comprehending the situation we currently found ourselves in. Or more accurately, the situation I now found myself in. The fact I had an evil ghost relative was terrifying enough but the fact that she remains on Earth specifically to look for her dead kids combined with the fact that she now thinks I'm one of those dead kids sent chills up my spine.

I stayed for a bit to talk about it all before deciding to call it a night and go home for dinner. After which I promptly forgot all about my little encounter with the dead and swiftly fell asleep.

The next morning I felt strange, as if something had disturbed me in the night but I wasn't sure what. I have quite an elaborate security system set up all over my house, garden and drive way so I decided to watch back the footage and investigate, wondering if I had been suffering a night terror or sudden bout of sleep paralysis…

I'd fallen asleep around 11:30pm. By 3:00am, nothing at all interesting had happened. I had rolled over in my sleep a few times and gotten up for the bathroom once but that was it. As the time got close to 4:00am, I began to notice a puddle forming in the top left hand corner of one of the screens. The footage from my driveway had something going on in it… I peered closer, noticing the bottom of a white dress just behind the puddle, as if a woman were standing in it just out of view…

It wasn't raining last night. I'm sure of it.

Just as I began to question my eyesight, the owner of the white dress stepped forward into view, allowing herself to be seen on another camera – the one outside my front door.

"No…" I breathed. It can't be.

La Llorona.

How did she find me?

I fast forwarded through the tapes and watched her as she glided through the doors of my home, floating up the stairs and into my bedroom. I watched her watch me as I slept…

Holding back my terror I kept watching the footage, seeing myself wake up with her still by my bed side, staring straight at me with outstretched arms. How hadn't I noticed her? How had I not sensed something?

Where was she now…?

I clicked out of the recorded footage and into live viewing, scanning my house for her presence. She was no longer in my bedroom, or the kitchen, or the drive way or garden. I searched every room from my computer, searching for the ghost of my dead relative, but she was nowhere to be found.

"Maybe she's gone?" I thought.

Feeling a cold chill down my spine, I realized there was still one room I hadn't checked;

The one I was in.

# Bunny Man Bridge

I didn't believe the stories at first. You know what people are like; they tell you things just to scare you – well that's exactly what I thought it was, just a story.

It doesn't sound scary does it – the 'bunny man'. If anything it just sounds like a cartoon character from an old TV show for under 5's, but if you're ever in West Virginia and you decide to take the short cut beneath Colchester overpass at night...

Don't.

My name is Don. I was about 14 when we moved here. My parents got a divorce and so mum, my brother Antony and I moved in to a little two bedroom apartment just off St. Helena's corner. I joined St Mary's high school the following September and that's where I first heard the stories.

"He's an old crazy farmer..." they would say in the canteen. "He wears the bunny mask because he got in a horrific tractor accident and doesn't like people looking at his scars..."

Others told a different tale;

"It's not a mask, he's a demon and the bunny ears are a disguise for his horns..." they'd whisper in the corridors; theorizing about the old town legend.

It was all stupid kid's stuff – none of it even believable, let alone scary. There were so many variations of the story that I made trying to hear them all a kind of hobby. I'd always been interested in storytelling and these were the kinds of things that interested me, I thought about writing a blog about it or maybe filming a documentary... After a while I started noticing a few similarities in the stories. Allegedly, he always appeared on a Sunday night at 11:00pm. I was disappointed at that; 3am would have been a more 'spooky' time. The other similarity that caught my attention was the small, repeated detail that anyone who had ever seen the bunny man had died. The only person who lived was an old farmer by the name of 'Jude'.

Of course, I decided to go and pay him a visit.

Jude wasn't quite the 'old' man that they said he was. When I first arrived I thought he looked no more than 40 but as we got talking I realised why they called him old. The way he carried himself wasn't like that of a 40 year old man. He sat in a little armchair by the window with a blanket over his lap. The fire was on, and in front of it hung a little old fashioned clothes horse with a number of patterned socks hanging from it. A box of medication sat next to him behind a pot of tea and two stained mugs...

When I asked about the bunny man for the first time he simply stared sadly out of the window and ignored me until I left, but of course I didn't give up – I was too invested, I needed to know. It wasn't until the third or fourth time I visited him and with a lot of prompting, that he finally told me his tale...

"His name was Arthur." He began.

"Before he became the bunny man he was a farmer, he was well known around these parts."

Jude poured himself a cup of tea as he spoke, his small reading glasses slipping down his nose as the folded newspaper on his lap slid closer to the floor.

"It was a Sunday, sometime in June 73 I think. I was about your age. Arthur had been out late with some friends. As he was driving back to the farm, a little rabbit ran out in front of the car. Arthur tried to stop but he was too close. He hit it hard. As he stepped out of the truck he noticed a fox creeping out from the side of the road, it tried to get the injured rabbit but Arthur quickly chased it away. He picked up the rabbit and wrapped it in his coat, bringing it back to the farm to care for it."

I tried to picture it in my head, visualizing Arthur and his little rabbit patient as they drove...

Jude continued;

"We all thought that little rabbit was gonna' die, but it didn't. Arthur looked after it well, built a little hutch for it and everything. He was a good man. When the rabbit was well enough to leave, the little thing didn't want to go. It'd grown so attached to Arthur that it refused to go anywhere without him, used to follow him around everywhere he went. Arthur decided to keep his new friend around; his only concern was the foxes..."

Jude paused, taking a sip of his tea and gazing out of the window. I wanted to push him to keep going but I kept quiet and waited, not wanting to be rude. Sure enough, after a few moments of quiet contemplation, Jude carried on with his story.

"The mask he made himself. I think he did it with papier-mâché and an old jumper, but no one really knows. I was the first person to see him in it, right out there, in the fields."

He pointed to a spot out of the window, his wrinkled hand trembling slightly before dropping heavily onto his lap. He sighed.

"He had a rifle with him... a .223."

He paused, as if forgetting where he was at in the story.

"Why did he have the rifle?" I asked, trying to jog his memory.

Jude nodded.

"He was hunting the foxes. That's what the rabbit mask was for – to attract them. He wanted to keep his rabbit safe."

I smiled. Suddenly the bunny man didn't seem like a scary story at all. Arthur the farmer and his rabbit friend could have, in fact, made a wonderful children's book.

Jude raised an eyebrow at my smile as if to say 'don't get too excited.'

"That's how it started..." He said.

My heart sank as I realized there probably wasn't going to be a happy ending to this story.

"At first he just did it when he saw foxes snooping around. He'd put the mask on and sit outside, luring them in and then shooting them dead. He used to sell the skins and everything, made quite a bit for himself, but after a while, it became his addiction. Every day you'd see him with the bunny mask on, hanging about in them fields. People started to worry about him. I started to worry..."

"How long had you known him?" I asked. I couldn't help but wonder, it seemed like he knew Arthur quite well.

Jude sighed heavily, his gaze resting on the floor at his feet.

"All my life." He said.

"He was my brother."

An awkward silence came over us both, I felt like I shouldn't have asked. Jude's gaze shifted towards the window, as if looking for Arthur.

"What happened to him?" I asked hesitantly.

It was a few moments before he replied.

"A lot of young couples around these parts use the fields for picnics and bonfires. We don't usually ever catch them, but the rubbish they leave behind disturbs the soil so we know when they've been there. Arthur, being out in the fields all the time, started to catch them. Every now and again you'd hear a warning shot, by the time you'd counted to ten they'd be driving off into the distance. The farmers appreciated Arthur and his weird bunny mask. The young people, not so much. They started spreading rumours about him... telling the village he was a crazy man. People started coming around more, they wanted to see him in action – like he was some kind of entertainment."

I started to feel sorry for Arthur.

Jude pressed on.

"One night a group of kids lit a fire in the back fields, the ones near the woods. The flames got so high I could see them from here. They were playing music, being loud. Woke us all up... I had a look out the window and sure enough Arthur was making his way towards them, mask on and rifle in hand."

I leaned in, sensing we were reaching the end of the true Bunny Man tale and eager to hear what happened.

"He didn't fire any warning shots this time, I think he'd had enough... I heard their screaming as he ran at them, chasing them into the woods and out by the Colchester underpass. They got into a car and started to drive away, but Arthur couldn't let them go. He jumped out in front of them and shot at the car."

He paused, his eyes glazing over with tears.

"They hit him. Hit him bad."

I wanted to reach out and comfort him, tell him how sorry I was for his loss, but I didn't want to interrupt the story…

"He wasn't found until the next morning, still had the mask on and everything. I went to bed after I saw him chase them off into the woods. I should have stayed up to make sure he came back, but I didn't."

He took a sip of his tea and cleared his throat, looking out of the window again.

"Is it true, what they say about him appearing on Sunday's?" I asked, hoping I wasn't coming across as insensitive.

Jude stared at me, his small dark eyes narrowing as if to say 'you shouldn't have asked that.'

He sighed.

"No."

Jude's gaze once again drifted out of the window, as if searching for Arthur in the fields.

"Even though Arthur died, he never really left. His spirit hangs around, watching over the animals and warning the rabbits when foxes are nearby… He's their protector. When an animal on the farm dies, that's when he appears. He helps to guide them into the next world."

I nodded, understanding the importance of Arthur's role here.

"Kids around here came to understand that, even saw him a few times. That's when they started holding their séances…"

Jude rolled his eyes and lightly thumped the arm of his chair with his balled up fist.

"Stupid, stupid." He muttered, his eyes filling with tears.

I suddenly felt worried, as if I should leap up from my chair and comfort him, but I didn't. His anger was difficult to watch.

"They would lay rabbit traps, killing the innocent creatures just to try and summon Arthur so they had a ghost story to tell at school."

"That's terrible..." I resonated with Jude's anger. How anyone could kill an innocent creature just to try and get a glimpse at an old ghost is beyond me.

Jude sighed and shrugged sadly.

"They get what's coming to them..." He whispered.

"They all do."

I nodded, putting the pieces together.

"So how does he do it?" I asked.

Jude frowned, as if forgetting where he was in the story again.

"Do what?" He asked.

"How does he kill them?" I asked.

Jude paused. "The trespassers?"

I nodded. "Yes. The ones that try to summon him..."

"Ah..." Jude nodded. "He doesn't."

I frowned in confusion as Jude leaned in closer towards me, as if about to tell me a big secret.

"I do." He smiled, lifting the blanket to reveal a rifle propped up next to his leg.

# Google Earth

I'm a 'bit of a weirdo' my mum would say. One thing I like to do when I'm bored at work or at home is to look at Google Earth. I like exploring the forests and checking out haunted or abandoned places... It interests me.

So there I am one day just kind of scrolling about some supposedly haunted place in Nairobi, when I notice this group of people all standing around a car in a circle. They had their arms raised and were wearing these long black cloaks... Google Earth blurs out faces so I couldn't see their expressions but somehow, they were all turned to face me, no matter what angle I viewed them at.

A few days later I was exploring some old Mayan pyramids in Mexico when I saw them again, the same group of cloaked, faceless figures standing in a circle around a rock. At first I didn't believe it but then I zoomed in... It was unmistakable. I didn't understand it, how could they be here too? I stared at the image for a while, to spooked to look away. Even though their faces were again blurred, I could feel their eyes staring straight into my soul.

I told a friend at work about the images I'd been finding; Gordon – he likes Google Earth too and wanted me to send him some screenshots. I promised him I'd try but I couldn't find the group the next few times I looked. It wasn't until about a week later that I saw them again.

I was checking out a place fairly close to me, an abandoned building surrounded by woodlands that were apparently well known for UFO sightings. As I scrolled across the landscape I saw them, standing in a circle around a small, rusting bicycle. I froze, wondering what they were doing so close to me?

Not wanting to look at the image for too long – I quickly took a screenshot and sent it to Gordon, promptly closing the laptop down and heading up to bed.

In the morning I woke to a text from my friend.

"That's so crazy!" It read. "Weird how they're all looking at the camera…"

I waited until I got to work to speak to him about it properly.

He wasn't in.

He didn't come in the next day either.

I tried calling him but there was no answer. I text him too but got no response.

The next night I went back on Google Earth, deciding to type in Gordon's address – I'm not sure why, I guess he was just on my mind.

As the camera zoomed in to Gordon's street and stopped above his house, I noticed something strange; a group of people nearby, in long, hooded cloaks.

I froze, my eyes wide with fear. How could it be?

I quickly dialled his number with my shaking, sweating fingers.

No answer.

I called him again.

This time I heard something… a phone ringing.

It was coming from my back garden.

I put my phone on the table and walked towards my back door, my knees quivering and my heart racing. I could barely breathe as I leant up against the cold glass and looked outside.

In front of me was a pair of eyes staring straight back through the glass. I jumped back in shock, realizing the second I did who it was.

"Gordon?" I asked quietly, pressing my nose back against the glass and looking out into the dark.

He was gone.

I took a few steps backwards, wondering if I had really just seen Gordon in my back garden or if I was going mad and hallucinating?

I decided on the latter, the first option was just too unrealistic. Why would Gordon be in my back garden after not answering his phone all day? He was obviously just unwell or away with some kind of family emergency...

The next day was my day off. I spent most of it shopping and cleaning before sitting down to relax and play some video games. After that... Well, I think you know what I did.

I went back on Google Earth. At first it was just to check Gordon's house again to see if what I saw before was still there... It wasn't.

Then I typed in my address.

I regretted it as soon as I did.

Sure enough, as the camera zoomed in on my street and I found my house, I saw the circle of people in cloaks standing in my back garden with their arms raised...

Only this time, there was one extra member.

My poor friend Gordon...

# The Ticking in the Walls

I was new to the city. Two suitcases of belongings a radio and a credit card in someone else's name was all I had. I wasn't planning on staying here long, the apartment I was renting was too small and the roof leaked. I had a friend in Chicago, she'd been telling me for weeks to head over and rent her spare room – I was planning on it, I just wanted to get some money behind me first. I had a good job here, good enough to put $50 a week or so into my savings account and still buy my food and pay my rent. Besides, I liked living alone, I could be a slob and there was no one around to judge me, but I'll admit, it does get lonely sometimes. Chicago is going to be fun, but for now – New York is just going to have to do.

Tuesday was by far my least favourite day off the week. My mum died on a Tuesday, our cat had gone missing on a Tuesday and now the girl I've liked for the last four months is changing her Tuesday shift for a Thursday – which means I have to go a full day at work without her. I contemplated changing my shift for a Thursday too but decided against it at the last minute - I'd look much too desperate. Instead, I decided I would just do my weekly shop on a Thursday from now on, I could check out at her till and make polite conversation, get her used to my presence and then one day I won't show up – then she'll miss me and that'll be my chance to ask her out. I smile at my plan on the bus ride home, 'anything worth having take's time' my mum used to say. Ria was worth having, even if it was just once before I left for Chicago.

I got home about 8pm, but I didn't notice it until gone 9. It was like whispers coming from the walls and the scuttling of little feet. At first I passed it off as the people next door, but then I realized it was in all the walls, in every room. I thought I was going crazy, I opened all the windows and looked around, wondering if there was a concert going on down the road I was unaware of that was causing some sort of hissy background noise – there wasn't. I checked the radio to see if it was coming from that, but it had been off the entire time. I was starting to get nervous, what the hell was it? Then, as suddenly as I'd noticed it, it stopped. It was the first time something like that had happened, but I should have taken the warning sign and left.

A few days later I was walking home from a friends, she only lived a few minutes away so I wasn't bothered about being out so late on my own. It was about 2am and I'd had a few glasses of wine, nothing too heavy. I heard a ticking. Like someone was flicking their tongue against their teeth over and over again, I looked around but saw no one. I picked up my pace but the noise followed close behind me, getting louder and louder. I broke into a run, sprinting towards my building and then slamming the door behind me, running up the stairs as fast as I could. I reached my apartment out of breath and panting, looking around nervously in case whatever had been following me was in the building. I shuddered thinking about it and opened my front door.

The roof had been leaking again; the ceiling was dark and bulging and a small puddle sat on the floor below it. I sighed, heading into the kitchen to get some tissues and a bucket. It wasn't long before I was in my usual spot on the sofa, flicking through the channels under my blanket, snacks and a drink on the table next to me. The world outside was dark and I had all but forgotten the ticking noise from earlier. I'd settled on watching an episode of some talk show and had been enjoying the first fifteen minutes of it before I heard it again. The ticking...

It was coming from outside my front door. I turned slowly to face it and stared.

Tick.

Tick.

Tick.

I froze.

Tick.

Tick.

Tick.

I realized I was holding my breath...

Tick.

Tick.

Tick.

What the hell is that? Why is it following me? I pull my knees up to my chest and sit in silence. Staring at the front door and hoping to God it would give up and leave me alone.

Tick.

Tick.

Tick...

It stopped... I exhaled as quietly as I could and held my hand up to my mouth, feeling the wetness on my cheek. I didn't even notice I had been crying... I reached for my phone and called Holly, a girl friend who lived downstairs. My hands were shaking as I held the phone to my ear and whispered:

"Please come..."

Holly sounded concerned. "I'll be right up, are you ok?" She asked.

I could hear her fumbling with her door chain already, she probably hasn't even put shoes on.

I shook my head. "I don't know, I just need you..."

"I'm coming."

I heard her run up the stairs and got up to open the door, waiting until I knew she was right outside.

Holly was the first person I met when I moved here, in fact she'd helped me get this place – before it I'd been staying in a hotel near where she works. Her bar was the first place I had a drink at.

"I'm outside babe." She called from the other side of the door, knocking twice.

I opened the door and reached out for her, hugging her tightly.

"What happened?" She asked, folding her arms around me and guiding me inside. She closed the door behind us and put the chain on as I sat back down in my spot on the sofa.

"I think I'm hearing things... A little while ago it was voices in the wall and now I'm being followed by something ticking... It followed me home, and then it was outside my door..." I started shaking. Holly came over and sat beside me, putting her arm around my shoulders and pulling me in for another cuddle. I sobbed in her chest.

"I'm going crazy." I cried.

"Shh, no you're not. Calm down, I'm sure there's reasonable explanations for it all."

I nodded, sitting back up and sniffing. "I know... I just can't find one." I stared at her, hoping she might hazard a guess. She stroked my arm and smiled.

"How about a drink, hmm? Take the edge off?"

I nodded as she got up and headed to my kitchen, taking out two wine glasses and poring us both a drink.

"If you want I could give you the number for my therapist... it helps to talk about these things sometimes, you know?"

I scoffed. "And get pumped full of medication? No thanks."

Holly laughed. "That's not what she's there for, it's just to get it all out and help find out what's going on or how to deal with it, you know?"

I nodded as she handed me my wine, I was pretty anxious about the whole thing. It couldn't hurt to just speak to someone.

"I know. I've never had therapy before, I don't want to suddenly find out I'm schizophrenic or something."

We both giggled. It felt good to laugh, I felt better, like I had nothing in the world to be worried about. But then we stopped, and I was back to facing reality – I was hearing things. If that wasn't a sign I was going mental I don't know what is. I leaned back on the sofa and sighed.

"I don't want to find out I'm crazy."

"You won't." Holly reassured me as she sipped her drink. "You'll probably just find out you're over-tired or watching too much TV or something." She laughed.

I nodded, looking over to the TV. That talk show was still on. I cocked my head to the side; I've seen this one before. I feel like I see it all the time...

"I started going to my therapist because of stress from work – we had a couple of bar fights that ended pretty badly, for both the people involved and the pub itself. I kept getting these dreams of people throwing petrol bombs through the windows, I'd be trapped in the fire and could feel myself burning up. But I couldn't die. I didn't even pass out from the smoke, I just stood there, feeling every second of my burning skin peel away..."

I stared at her. "Jesus... That sounds rough."

She nodded. "I'd wake up coughing and sweating, needing to lean out a window or splash cold water in my face, you know... Anxiety, that's what it was – but it had nothing to do with the pub – it turns out I was already anxious about things that happened way before, my brain was just using the pub scenario and circumstance to let it all out."

I nodded. "Wow. What was the thing?"

She frowned, as if she didn't get what I meant by the 'thing'.

"The thing you were anxious about, that happened before..." I felt awkward clarifying. I was re-thinking my decision in even asking in the first place – it really wasn't my business knowing. I hadn't even known her that long.

She smiled.

"My parents were murderers."

I stared at her, she didn't say anything else.

"Shit... That must have been hard when you found out."

"I knew all along." She smiled again, as if she were proud of it. "They told me everything, I knew what they were doing – I just didn't think it was bad, they told me it was ok..."

I shuddered. I'd heard about that kind of brain washing technique happening with kidnappers, or people who wanted to raise child terrorists... It was weird to know someone I know had suffered it.

"Did you ever see it happen?" I asked. I couldn't help myself.

"Always."

I did what Holly said and saw the therapist – our first session wasn't much, it was just her getting to know me. But my second session was quite something. For starters it began with a glass of champagne...

"So, what are we celebrating?" I asked as she clanked her champagne glass against mine, the liquid bubbling away.

She smiled. "The start of your new life, I am going to change you Sarah, I'm going to give you back control of your life. Does that sound like something you're ready to drink to?"

I smiled and took a sip. "Well cheers to that."

We sat down and began speaking, firstly about what I wanted to do with my life, then about the whispering in the walls and the ticking. There had been a few more instances where I'd felt like I was being watched or someone was in the room with me but I didn't quite feel ready to mention those. We'd almost finished when she gave me a task.

"How secure is your building Sarah?"

I shrugged. "Pretty secure, the door has a key entry system and there's security camera's on every floor."

She leaned in as if about to tell me a secret.

"So tonight, when you go home, I want you to try something, a kind of spiritual exercise..."

I nodded, intrigued to hear what she was talking about.

"I want you to turn off all appliances, sit cross legged on the floor of your front room and leave your door unlocked, for one whole hour. Sounds strange right?"

I nodded, waiting for her to elaborate.

"The purpose of this," she continued, "is to learn to let go of control. As humans we have this compulsive need to try and control everything, by locking our doors we control the risk factor for danger and block anything unwanted from entering our space. You are scared something is trying to get in, so leave the door unlocked; invite it in. If it comes in, you can deal with it – if nothing happens – it is all in your head, and then we need to deal with that. You see?"

I smiled, I understood what she was trying to say. It was an interesting way of narrowing down the list of things that could be happening with me. A fun game of am I paranoid or do I actually have a stalker?

"But what if someone really is stalking me and they come in when the door is unlocked..." I asked.

"How will they know the door is unlocked?" She asked, half laughing.

I shrugged, how would they? It wasn't like I would be advertising it. I liked the idea of letting go of control though... I felt like I needed that, to let go of the constant pressure of being on task and schedule. Leave the door unlocked – it was so simple, yet kind of dangerous... I felt excited. Maybe it was the bubbly...

"If you're still unsure, just try for ten or fifteen minutes, you don't have to do the full hour."

I nodded, that sounded much better.

"If you like, tell me the time you plan to do it and I'll call after you're finished, we can talk through your feelings."

That sounded nice. It was good to have someone's support.

"I'll probably do it around 8pm." I smiled.

She made a note if it and grinned, "Perfect."


So there I was at 8pm, lighting candles and incense to create a calming atmosphere as per the therapist's advice. I stared at the front door, imagining the ticking noise behind it; taunting me. I took a deep breath and shook off the feelings of uneasiness as I asked for guidance from God and his angels. I put on some calming meditation music and a timer for 20 minutes; I wanted to start out small. When everything was ready, I took off the chain, bolt and turned the key – unlocking the front door completely.

Nothing happened.

No ticking, no stalker bursting in to kidnap me...

Maybe this was going to be ok.

I took my place on the floor of the living room and focused on my breathing, counting down from 100. It wasn't long before I started day dreaming, first about my life back home, my parents and friends, then about work, projects I had been working on and wanted to work on in the future... I decided I liked meditation; I could think about anything, I could be anywhere and do anything. Wanting to explore a little further I started to visualize myself in ten years time; the kind of house I wanted to be living in and job I wanted to be doing... I smiled to myself as imagined the older me walking through her big house in Chicago, with its fancy décor and dark oak furnishings. I'd have a room entirely dedicated to art and a huge balcony overlooking a forest. Are there forests in Chicago? My vision feels so real I can hear the busy street below, the whispering of the wind and the ticking of the clock behind me... I picture myself standing on the balcony of my beautiful house, looking out at the world beyond mine and breathing in the fresh air. I can feel the wind on my face...

I wonder how long it's been since I began meditating and decide I'm going to open my eyes in a moment, I just want to take it all in before I do...

Tick.

Tick.

Tick.

Then it hits me. The whispering of the wind wasn't just in my vision; the ticking of the clock was something else entirely... I needed to open my eyes, it's here.

My eyes flicked open just at the timer I set on my phone went off, making my jump and almost scream. My front door was wide open and swinging and the whispering and ticking had suddenly stopped. I jumped up to close the door, locking it quickly and sitting down on the sofa, wrapping a blanket around me. I remembered what the therapist had said and waited for her call, but it didn't come. After a while I must of drifted off because the next thing I knew it was pitch black and the ticking was back. I sat up slowly, wrapping the blanket tighter around myself as a cold breeze whipped my ankles. I had no idea what the time was.

"Come closer…" Came a whisper from the wall to my left. I turned to face it, my face scrunched in confusion.

"What?" I murmured as I edged forward. "What are you?"

"Come and join us, come closer…" It continued. I froze on the spot, begging for someone to come rushing in through the door to save me. Why hadn't the therapist called? I decided to call her and pulled my phone from my pocket, backing away from the wall and searching for a light switch with my free hand.

"Sarah, good to hear from you – how did it go?" She asked cheerily.

"There's something in my house." I whispered.

"Now, are you quite sure?" She asked.

"Yes…"

Something didn't feel right; the phone call was odd, her voice echoed strangely.

"Ok, I want you to… kill… in the wall…" The line became sketchy, her voice was breaking up.

"I can't hear you properly." I called. "Are you still there?"

"And the lover of blood shall cleanse them, and the lover of blood shall cleanse them…" A warped, deep voice came from the handset, shrouded in white noise. I brought my hand to my mouth and dropped the phone, I could feel myself shaking violently. I needed to get out. I ran to put my shoes on and heard it, coming from behind the front door.

Tick.

Tick.

Tick.

It's waiting for me...

My knees became weak and I fell to the floor, helpless.

"What do you want?" I screamed, hoping I could give it something it wanted and it would leave me alone.

Tick.

Tick.

Tick.

It continued without hesitation. I crawled backwards away from the door and hid behind the sofa, praying this was all a terrible dream.

"Come to us..." The walls whispered. "We'll protect you."

The ticking was getting louder, faster and closer to the door, I imagined it would soon pass straight through it and I would have nowhere to run.

"What's happening?" I begged the walls for answers but they simply repeated themselves.

"Come to us..."

I nodded, defeated and crawled slowly towards them. Reaching out to touch them just as the ticking noise crossed the door. I didn't see it all, just the huge blackness that came with it, a shadow creature, reaching out to save me. The last thing I remember is hearing a quiet laughter as I fell into a deep sleep.

When I woke up I was here, on the other side. A parallel world on the other side of these very walls...

# The Lady at 305

"Listen... Can you hear the music?" She whispered, leaning forward in her chair.

Gina was old, should she live another 5 years she'll be getting a birthday card from the Queen. I'd been working for her for about a month now and was used to her nonsensical ramblings. She heard and seen a lot of things that weren't there and as usual, I nodded and played along.

"I do... Isn't it wonderful?" I smile, tucking a blanket over her lap and wiping the tea from her chin with a tissue.

"It's glorious. They've been playing all day that band, what are they called again?"

"I can't remember." I say, taking a seat next to her and picking up the Radio Times. "There's a documentary on channel 4 later about sealife..."

"Brass bands they call them, because of the instruments they use, I think... Brass... I have some brass plates over there." She pointed to a small cabinet in the corner by the kitchen, coated in a patterned cloth and decorated with silver photo frames and a small cactus.

"That's cool. Where did you get them?"

She looked at me confused for a moment, as if forgetting what we had just been talking about – which was actually something that happened on a pretty regular basis.

"Some market somewhere... You look familiar. Have we met before?"

I giggled, reaching out for her hand. "Yes Gina, I'm your carer."

It was always like that. She had been diagnosed with dementia a few years back and recently had been getting much worse, at least twice a visit she'd ask who I was and she couldn't remember my name if her life depended on it.

"Don't talk to the woman at 305." She whispered. "She's crazy… Crazy old lady."

I laughed. "That's not very nice, why is she crazy?"

"She'll kill you." She replied, her voice low and serious. "Kill you dead."

I frowned and nodded, patting her hand to reassure her I wasn't about to go knocking at the crazy lady at 305.

"Don't you worry."

The next day was my day off. I've been taking a course in business management so used the free time to study and relax, that's what Sunday's are for, right?

The day after that I was back at Gina's. It was about 10am when I got there for my first shift, hoovering and washing up. She asked me to organize some books for her and straighten her bed – which I did, of course. It was the last thing she asked me to do that had me a little confused.

"Take this…" She said, holding out an envelope towards me. "Post it at number 305 before you go."

I raised an eyebrow as I took it. "I thought you didn't like the woman at 305?"

Gina looked up at me, glaring as if angry that I could suggest such a thing.

"I never said that." She whispered.

That was true, but she did call her crazy…

"Oh, sorry. My mistake."

I posted the envelope through number 305's letterbox on my way home, wondering what Gina would be writing to her about. It wasn't close to Christmas, maybe it was her birthday? Old people are like that; even if they hate each other they'll still send a birthday card each year. I forgot all about it within about five minutes and went home. A few hours later I was back for the evening shift.

"Hello love." I smiled walking back into Gina's small, one bedroom flat. There was no answer. I assumed she was in the loo and began hanging out the clean washing while I waited for her. After five minutes she still hadn't appeared. I stepped into the hall and knocked on the bathroom door.

"Gina." I called, loudly. "Are you ok?"

Still no answer.

I tried the door handle, realizing it wasn't locked. "I'm coming in" I called, opening the door and popping my head round the frame. She wasn't there.

I stepped back into the hall and checked the bedroom. She wasn't there either.

"Shit." I muttered.

We've had clients go missing before, especially the dementia sufferers. It happens more often than you'd think – their minds go wandering and suddenly they're in their 40's again and going out for lunch with Tim and Harry from the office, next thing you know they're hobbling up and down Kilburn High Road in their slippers with no idea how they got there. I ran into the front room and took out Gina's address book from a drawer and called John – her son and emergency contact.

"Hiya Mum." He answered quickly, assuming it was Gina calling for an early evening chat since I was calling off of her house phone.

"Hey John, it's Kumbi…" I began.

"Oh, hello." He was surprised to hear my voice, we hadn't really spoken since I'd started working for his mother. "Is everything ok?"

"Well, I don't want to worry you but it seems Gina has gone for a little wander… Do you have any idea where she might have gone?"

He paused for a moment, sighing loudly.

Oh Lord. He's panicking. I should have looked around for her before calling him… She's probably just gone outside and sat in the garden, now I've got him all worked up for nothing. I raised my hand to my forehead, getting annoyed at myself for acting so quickly and not taking a moment to assess the situation properly. I've been doing this job for years now – I should have thought to check the ground and knock at neighbours before jumping on the phone. John was taking a while to speak…

"John?" I said gently as I headed over to the window to check outside. "Are you ok?"

"Yeah." He said, unconvincingly. "I'm ok, stay where you are I'll be there in a minute."

I hesitated. "Oh, it's ok – if you know where she is I can just go and get her?"

"No." His reply came quickly. "I know where she is, just, it's… just wait for me."

I frowned, not understanding why he was being so vague but agreed to wait for him. He ended the call by telling me not to knock at the neighbours…

I decided to check around the garden to see if I could find her while I waited for John. It was a big garden that went around the entire block. I couldn't see the whole thing from Gina's small front room windows. I took the stairs instead of the lift so that I could look down the hallways and check if she was wandering another floor. She wasn't.

By the time I got outside it had been about five minutes, she could be anywhere. I was starting to worry… After my first walk around the garden I knew she wasn't there, but I walked around a second and third time just to be sure, peeking over the hedges to check the roads.

I could see John's car pulling into the carpark and headed over to meet him, still keeping lookout for Gina.

"Hey." He patted me on the shoulder as he greeted me. "Still not back?"

I shook my head. "I've just done a few laps of the garden but I can't find her anywhere."

I tried not to sound as worried as I was.

"Come with me." He said, using his key card to get into the building.

I followed him, thinking we were going back up to her apartment to call the police. Instead we stopped a few doors down...

Outside number 305.

He turned to face me before knocking. "Do you know if she posted a letter here recently?"

I frowned. "She did, she asked me to do it... Why?"

He took a breath and knocked.

"Just... stay with me."

I nodded slowly. "She said the woman that lived here was crazy..." I whispered.

John chuckled. "She is."

The door unlocked but didn't open. John stood there for a moment, counting to five out loud before he pushed the door open and entered. I followed him inside.

"Close the door." He whispered. I did as he instructed, hovering behind him as we edged forward into the dark and empty flat.

"9415." He called, pulling out a .44 mag. "Answer yes if you can understand me."

A low growl could be heard coming from a room off to the left.

"Jesus Christ, what's going on?" I whispered loudly, unable to control the confusion showing in my quivering and unnaturally squeaky voice.

"Shh..." John replied. "Don't make any sudden moves, and keep quiet."

I froze.

"9415, say yes if you can understand me..."

"Yessss..." A faint reply croaked from behind the half open door.

John edged closer to the room. "Good." He said, shooting me a reassuring nod.

It wasn't very reassuring at all. I was petrified.

"What's your status?" He called out.

"I'm... Changing..." Came the croaky reply.

I held my breath as John reached the door, the revolver stretched out in front of him.

"How long?" He asked, pushing the door open.

A foul stench filled the room. I gasped and stepped back, holding my hand over my nose.

"Stay right there. Don't... Move..." John swayed, crumpling to the floor as the creature crawled out of the room, stepping over his body.

In my head, I screamed. Physically, I must have followed Johns lead because the next thing I remember he was waking me up and it was a few hours later...

"Kumbi..." He shook me gently as my eyes fluttered open.

"W... what happened?" I stammered, looking around for the creature.

"How are you feeling?" He asked.

I stood up and dusted myself off, noticing the half open front door.

"I'm... confused. What the hell happened?"

He sighed and scratched his head.

"Well – it's a little hard to explain. I'm not Gina's son, I'm her handler."

"I'm sorry, you're her what?" I frowned, more confused than ever.

"Her handler, or at least I was. Gina is what we call her while she's in human form... Have you heard the term 'lycanthrope' before?"

I raised an eyebrow. "Lycan... Like werewolf?"

He nodded.

"Well, yes. Kind of, I mean, it's not what you think."

I folded my arms in a 'try me' kind of way.

"Ok." John smiled. "If you really want to know... Gina is part of a protection program for human sub-species. Most of her kind live in underground caves and forests, we help them integrate into society should they want to, and provide the care they need when they get older. They're still half human; they still deteriorate and suffer like the rest of us. They still have rights."

I shook my head, not quite believing anything he was saying.

"I know how it sounds, trust me. We used to have our own specially trained carers but the government cut funding to our program so now we have to rely on the ones the council provide and just hope they don't have an episode in their presence..."

"What's an episode?" I asked.

"Like when a werewolf changes on a full moon."

I nodded. "Oh…"

"That's what this place is for, 305. All the Lycanthropes we work with are given two flats; one to live in as a human, and one to lock themselves in when they 'change'."

His story was starting to take shape, but it still didn't sound real.

"So… where is she now?" I asked.

He shrugged. "As they get older they start to change more and more frequently until they die. They can't control it. When they die, they rarely die as a human. They always know when it's there time to go and they do it as an animal, away from people, in a forest or somewhere peaceful."

"You mean she's gone to die?" I asked, horrified at the way he was talking about it so casually.

He nodded sadly. "The gas she let off before she left – the one that knocked us out, that's something that happens just before they go. It's her time."

My hand instinctively raised to my mouth to hide the gasp I'd let out picturing her rotting, half-animal corpse in a forest somewhere… She wouldn't have a funeral. No grave we could visit.

"But… she…" I couldn't finish my sentence.

"It's ok, it happens all the time." He smiled. "Not quite like this. Ideally we would have sedated her and taken her to a facility where she could be incinerated, but enough about Gina, let's talk about your future."

I frowned. "My future?"

"Well, I have plenty of other clients needing short term carers for their final days and it would be nice to have someone knowledgeable about their 'condition.' What do you think?"

I didn't know what to say. I just stood there, staring at him. Was he serious? Was this all just some huge, weird and elaborate prank? The room spun.

"You don't have to answer right now, take a few days to think about it. Here, take my card." He said, handing me a business card as we headed towards the front door to leave.

I took it as he bent down to pick up the letter I had dropped through the door earlier that day, exhaling loudly as he opened it. It was a postcard, with a picture of a forest in autumn on the front. He smiled and turned it over.

"Thanks for everything. G." It read.

# Slenderman

He didn't lock the door that night. I know because I heard him come in, he ran straight into the kitchen and turned on the tap – I guess to sober up before coming to bed. He'd been drinking more and more recently, I blamed myself for his relapse. After he came out of rehab I promised to help keep him away from our local by dragging him off to yoga and patchwork classes with me to keep him occupied. He never came, and I never persisted. Our relationship was coming to an end anyway, he knew it – I knew it, we just didn't want to face it. So whenever he hopped off to the pub to drown his sorrows, I let him. I liked the alone time more than I did time with him. It gave me space to think, to focus on my own work and goals.

"Jordan?!" He called. I rolled my eyes and turned over, not in the mood for conversation.

"Jord!" He was running up the stairs now, probably eager to tell me who'd won the game or some other news I had no interest in.

"Jordan!" He threw the door open and ran in, kneeling beside me and shaking me awake. I wasn't asleep, I was just pretending to be in the hope he'd leave me alone. I sighed and opened my eyes.

"What?" I grumbled, annoyed with his presence and not caring about hiding it.

"I saw him…" He whispered.

I raised an eyebrow and propped myself up on the pillow.

"Saw who?"

"Slenderman."

I groaned.

"For God's sake, Nathan, you're drunk."

"I'm not!" He protested.

He was lying, I could smell it on his breath.

"Ok." I didn't care to argue with him.

"So you saw Slenderman. Are you sure it wasn't just a tall, skinny guy?"

I reached for my pack of cigarettes on the bedside table and lit one up, taking a long drag as Nathan argued his case.

"It was Slenderman, ok. I know what I saw. He was over 12 feet tall!"

I nodded and raised both eyebrows sarcastically.

"I'm sure…"

Nathan was getting irritated at my lack of interest but I didn't care. If anything I think I wanted to piss him off, I wanted him to get so annoyed with me he packed a bag and left. I didn't have the energy for him anymore.

"What is your problem?" He asked, his voice getting louder with his dampening mood.

"You." I replied, unable to tame my annoyance.

"You, are my problem. After everything that's happened you're drinking again."

"I'm not drunk!" He yelled.

"You're a liar." I yelled back. I didn't want a shouting match at this time of night but if he was about to take it there I wasn't going to back down.

He paused before responding.

"Ok, I had two beers – but I'm not drunk."

I scowled and flicked the covers off of me, standing up and leaving the room.

"Where are you going?" He called after me.

I turned back around and glared at him from the doorway.

"Anywhere you're not."

I went downstairs and into the kitchen, pouring myself a large glass of wine and sitting at the table to finish my cigarette. It wasn't long before Nathan followed me, raising his eyebrow at my wine.

"Oh, so you can drink…"

"I wasn't an alcoholic, Nath." I interrupted, a little harsher than I intended.

He stopped and looked down sheepishly at his feet.

"Sorry..." He mumbled.

I wasn't buying it, he was always sorry.

"I can't keep doing this." I said sadly, looking away from him. I didn't want to cry but I could feel the tears welling up behind my eyes. I really was at the end of my tether.

"I just... I don't know what more I can do..."

He nodded, taking a step forward and sitting down beside me.

"I promise, I'm not drunk... I swear I only had two beers..."

"I don't care Nath." I interrupted.

"I really don't. Do what you like but you're not dragging me down with you anymore."

He frowned, confused.

"Wait... Are you breaking up with me?" He asked.

I sighed loudly.

"I don't know..."

I wanted to, but I still loved him...

He took my hand. I think it was the first time he'd held my hand in weeks...

"Jord..." He whispered.

"Please look at me."

I looked up reluctantly, knowing if I looked into those deep blue eyes I wouldn't be able to look away.

"I'm sorry... I'll make it better, whatever it is we can work through it..."

I shook my head.

"You always say that, but nothing ever changes..."

"Please..." He whispered.

"I can't lose you too."

I knew he was going to play that card… He'd lost both his parents a few years back and anytime things got hard he would pull out the old 'You're all I have left' speech…

"If you lose me it's because that's what you chose. I've told you countless times this can't continue and if it does I'm walking away. How many more chances do you think I can give you before I actually do walk away?!"

I pulled my hand away from him and stood up, downing my wine and slamming the glass back down on the table.

"Fix up, or I'm gone."

He nodded sadly as the phone rang. I shot him a look before answering, as if it was his fault we were being disturbed at such a late hour.

"Hello?" I huffed.

"Hendrix is missing. Please come…"

I froze. It was Nathan's half-sister Julia; Hendrix was her son.

"Shit… We'll be right there. Hang tight." I said before putting the phone down and grabbing my coat.

"What is it?" Nathan asked.

I took a deep breath before telling him, I wasn't sure how he'd take it.

"Hendrix is missing…" I said softly.

He stared at me for a minute, as if he hadn't heard what I had said.

"M…Missing?" He repeated, picking his keys up from the kitchen table.

"Don't even think about it." I snapped. "I'm driving."

He nodded, putting his keys back down and following me out the front door.

Julia didn't live far – about a ten minute drive, but with the empty roads we were there in close to five.

"What happened?" I asked as Julia collapsed into my arms. She was sobbing her heart out and could barely speak. I took her into her front room and sat her down, instructing Nathan to make her a large coffee. Julia and I were much closer than she was to Nathan. She still hadn't forgiven him for a few things he'd put his family through whilst dealing with his addiction. I didn't blame her to be honest, he'd royally screwed up on a number of occasions.

"He said he was coming... He said it , he kept saying it... Why didn't I listen..." She cried into my chest as I rubbed her back.

"What do you mean?" I asked, confused. "Who's coming?"

"He kept drawing him and showing me, telling me he was coming to get him but I just thought it was a game or a bad dream... I should have taken him seriously, why didn't I listen?!" She was hysterical now.

I had no idea what she meant but I didn't want to pester her for more information while she was like this. I had to calm her down, she wasn't thinking straight.

"Ok... It's ok we'll find him, don't worry..." I soothed, holding her close and stroking her hair – trying to be as comforting as I could. I didn't really know how to comfort a woman. Did they like their hair being stroked? I had no idea.

"I saw him..." Nathan said quietly as he placed a large coffee on the table for Julia. He had a piece of paper in his hands that looked like one of Hendrix's drawings...

"You saw him?" Julia asked desperately.

Nathan nodded, not looking her in the eye and taking a seat in the armchair opposite.

"I didn't... I didn't think he... I thought I was imagining things..."

"Was Hendrix with him?" She whispered.

"I don't know..."

I frowned, not knowing what or who they were on about.

"Hold up..." I said, keeping my hand firmly on Julia's back and trying to remain as comforting as I could. "Who are you talking about?"

Nathan took a deep breath before sliding the drawing over the coffee table to me.

I froze, recognizing the pencil figure almost immediately.

"Slenderman." Nathan said quietly.

"Where did you see him?" Julia asked as I picked up the paper in my shaking fingers. It couldn't be...

"He was standing at the edge of the woods... By Rimell's Farm..."

I shook my head, not wanting to believe Nathans drunken ramblings had been anything other than just that; drunken ramblings. There was no way in hell 'Slenderman' had taken Hendrix. He was just folklore, imaginary, right?

"We have to go. We have to go and find him." Julia stood up quickly, pulling on a heavy winters coat and wrapping a scarf around her neck.

"I'll get some torches." Nathan nodded, heading into the kitchen.

"Hold up... You guys really believe Slenderman took Hendrix?"

"Yes." Julia replied, staring at me hard as if not believing in the local urban legend was a symptom of insanity.

I didn't have a response. I just stared at her back as Nathan reappeared in the doorway with a hand full of torches.

"It can't hurt to try..." He shrugged, nodding in a weak reassurance at his half-sister.

I sighed, realizing how my 'reasoning' could come across as insensitive at a time like this. "Sorry... Of course, you're right. I'll drive..."

Nathan wrapped his arm around Julia as we left, helping her into the car.

We pretty much drove in silence, I could feel the both of them staring out at the roads for any sign of little Hendrix. He would be turning 7 this May and the dark, winding roads were no place for a small child.

"What was he wearing?" Nathan asked.

"His blue coat... Jeans... White T-shit..." Julia mumbled, not taking her eyes off the road.

We arrived at Rimell's farm within about 5 minutes – luckily it wasn't too far away.

I decided to head over to the farm house and speak with the farmer to see if he had seen anything while Nathan and Julia headed off into the woods...

I knocked a number of times but no one came to the door, which was strange because lights were on and there were cars in the drive. I shouted through the letterbox but still no one answered.

Getting annoyed, and realizing time really was at the essence here – I decided to walk around the perimeter of the house to see if I could see anyone. As I reached the back door I caught a glimpse of the farmer in the kitchen. I knocked on the window but he didn't look up.

"What the hell?" I muttered to myself, knocking a second time.

A few seconds later a young woman appeared at the side of the house and called me over, she didn't look any older than 15.

"Hey... Can I help you?" She asked.

I looked back towards the farmer in the kitchen.

"Uh... Yeah, I was hoping to speak to the owner of the farm?" I asked. She smiled.

"That's my dad... He's, a little difficult. What can I do for you?" She asked politely, insinuating that whatever it was that I needed, her father would take no interest.

I took a short breath before responding.

"It's my friend... Her son has gone missing, I was just wondering if you'd seen anything or if you..."

"Oh..." She sighed, looking anxiously over her shoulder to the woods.

"And... You want our help looking for him?"

I nodded. What a weird way to offer to help...

"Wait there..." She said, disappearing back inside of the house. I glanced nervously towards the woods, wondering what could have happened to Hendrix...

The young woman re-appeared a few moments later with a man, who I assumed was an older brother.

"This is Dean..." She said. "He'll help you."

I nodded, slightly confused but grateful for any help I could get.

The girl turned back towards the house, pausing before she entered.

"I'm sorry for your loss." She said quietly, heading inside and closing the door behind her.

"Loss?" I thought... What an odd way to word it. He was missing, not dead.

"So you've lost your kid." Dean said.

"Come with me..."

I followed him over to a tractor and watched him climb up.

"Get in." He instructed in a low, gruff voice. I nodded and climbed up the huge tire, taking a seat next to him.

"How long's he been missing for?" He asked, starting the engine and driving off towards the woods.

"I'm not sure..." I replied. "Maybe an hour or so?"

Dean nodded, not taking his eyes off of the dark, muddy fields in front of us. He didn't ask any more questions as we crossed the farm, stopping at the entrance to the woods.

I could see the lights of a few torches in the distance.

"That your friends?" Dean asked as he turned off the engine.

I nodded.

He exhaled loudly.

"They're not gonna find him."

I frowned. "Why would you say that?"

He sighed and looked down, as if about to tell me something absurdly difficult.

"Kids go missing around these parts a lot." He said quietly. "It's part of the reason my father brought this land... His little sister was taken too..."

"Taken?" I asked, noticing the change in his wording. "What do you mean taken?"

We climbed out of the tractor and began walking in the direction of the flashlights.

"It's not an easy story to tell." He began. "Back when I was a kid they called him Creeper, then it was The Grey Gentleman, then Mr Faceless, Skin and Bones man... He had a lot of names. It's only in the last few years people have started calling him… Well, I'm sure you've heard of him."

I raised an eyebrow. "You're not talking about…" I paused before saying his name. "Slenderman… Are you?"

He nodded, clearing his throat before speaking again.

"I know a lot of folks think it's just some urban legend, and in truth – we'd like to keep it that way."

I looked at him, his dusty blonde hair was feathered around his furrowed brow and a single buck tooth slipped out between his thick lips. Was I really about to take anything this man said as fact? I took his words with a pinch of salt, wondering how inbred his family where.

"It's not just one man though, Slenderman. The man in the stories – it's not the same one."

"It's not?" I asked.

He shook his head.

"People always think that. That it's just one, really tall guy that's been kidnapping youngsters at random every few years since their great-grannies can remember. But it's not, there's a whole colony of them…"

We kept on walking deeper into the woods, getting closer to Nathan and Julia as we spoke.

"Where… Who…" I couldn't get my words out…

"No one knows. They just appeared one day a couple hundred years ago, no one knows why or where they came from. There's a portal, in these woods… That's where they take the children…"

I stopped walking, not caring about how realistic it all sounded anymore.

"So, if we find the portal – we'll find Hendrix?" I asked, hopeful.

Dean stared at me with regret and sadness in his deep blue eyes.

"No." He said bluntly.

"Once they go through the portal… They never come back."

Suddenly, a blood curdling scream could be heard echoing through the darkness.

"Julia…" I whispered, taking off in the direction it came from. Dean followed closely behind.

"No!" She screamed again as we got closer, her sobs coming thick and fast in the dark silence.

"Julia!" I yelled as we got closer.

"Jordan?!" I could hear Nathan shouting for me. I watched the torchlight darting around the looming trees as he searched for me.

"Nathan!" I called back, picking up the pace as we approached the small circle of trees they were in the middle of. I could see Julia kneeling on the floor, cradling something in her arms…

Hendrix?

As we got closer I realized exactly what it was.

A small blue coat.

Hendrix's coat.

I fell to the floor and held her close, rocking her back and forth as she cried into my chest.

I turned to Dean, who was standing just outside the small circle of trees.

"Help us…" I pleaded with him. "We need to find that portal."

Dean hesitated before looking up at me, visibly disturbed.

"You just stepped through it…"

I looked up at the trees that surrounded us. Suddenly, the trunks no longer looked like normal tree trunks, and the branches no longer looked like branches. Instead, the trunks had become tall, slender legs in pin striped trousers, and the branches had turned into long, bony outstretched fingers…

# Viral

I took a pull of my cigarette and leant against the lamppost, waiting for Kayleigh's little fiesta to pull up. I hadn't seen her in a month or so and we'd finally found some time in our busy schedules to spend together. She was a nurse and I a healthcare assistant. We'd known each other for about 15 years.

"How's it going?" She asked as I climbed into the car, leaning in to give me a hug.

We went to get some food and then picked my sons up from school before heading back to mine to catch up properly. She hadn't seen my new house yet, I'd only just recently moved in and so I gave her the grand tour.

"It's so cute I love it!" She smiled, looking around my grey and black themed bedroom. "How much is it?"

I rolled my eyes, "Nearly two grand a month, but it's worth it for the studio space."

She nodded, "It definitely is. Housing in London is so expensive these days..."

"It is." I sighed. "How much are you paying in Essex?"

"Well we have a mortgage so it's a lot cheaper, a little over nine hundred a month."

Wow. That was much better. "And how many bedrooms is it?" I asked.

"Three."

"Nice."

We sat in the kitchen for a few hours and chatted over coffees while the boys played upstairs. It had just gone 6pm by the time she started heading home.

"Let me know when you're free to come and stay!" She smiled as we said our goodbyes.

"I will, drive safe."

The boys gave her a hug and waved goodbye from the driveway. It was a nice evening, the kind I wished we could have more of.

After that the boys and I got ready for bed. It was a Thursday, and I was looking forward to the weekend.

The next morning I got back from the school run a little later than usual, the traffic was pretty bad this morning – I'm guessing an accident had happened somewhere on the Edgware road due to the amount of Ambulances I'd seen, but I didn't hear anything about it on the radio. Once I got home I had a bath. I wasn't working that day and so I'd decided to pamper myself, I was planning on having a facial and doing my nails before I saw my phone.

Kayleigh – 8 missed calls.

I had a text from her too, it just said "Call me as soon as you see this."

I frowned and sat down to call her.

"Hey, what's up?" I asked as she answered the phone.

"Hey, I don't mean to worry you but there's been an outbreak of something at the hospital... I'm not sure what it is but it's some kind of virus." She sounded worried. "The whole wards been on quarantine since last night, I only just found out..."

"Oh..." I wasn't quite sure how to react.

"I'm just warning you because we had close contact yesterday, how are the boys, do they feel ok?"

"Yeah the boys are fine, they're at school – what kind of virus is it? What symptoms do I need to look out for?"

She paused.

"We're not sure yet... It's still being tested, apparently only a few patients and staff members have caught it so I wouldn't worry too much, just make sure to take some vitamins and drink lots of water."

"Ok, I will." I replied.

I decided it would probably be a good idea if I did some cleaning and started wiping down all the surfaces... I remembered Kayleigh sneezing at one point yesterday, was that a symptom or just allergies? I shrugged it off and began hoovering.

A few hours later I was on my way to pick up the boys, the traffic was awful again; barely moving. I decided to park up and walk, it wasn't too far away and I could walk pretty fast... I should have stayed in the car.

As I turned the corner to the school... Nearly every car had been abandoned. Some had crashed into each other, some had smoke coming from the engines. I could hear car and house alarms in the distance... What was happening? I had no idea.

I picked up the pace and kept on towards the school, noticing the crowd of parents standing outside the gate. Why wasn't it open yet? I checked the time, it should be open by now...

As I got closer I noticed the medical staff that were standing outside in masks talking to the parents closest to the gate, I pushed through the crowd to get closer.

"What is it, what's happening?" I asked.

"There's been an outbreak of something..." One parent replied.

"Some kind of virus." Another shouted over the noise of the crowd.

"Please, if you could all just remain calm we can get this sorted..." shouted a nurse.

I took out my phone and called Kayleigh.

"What's up?" She answered quickly.

"The boys school is on lock down, the virus is here too. What is it?" I asked in hushed tones.

"We don't know yet babe... We've had some more people come in with it, we're running every test possible I'll update you as soon as I know something, I really have to go ok. Just get the boys and get home."

I nodded and hung up, fighting my way to the front of the crowd again and grabbing one of the nurses in masks by the sleeve.

"Hey, I'm a Doctor," I lied, hoping it would get me in. "We've had an outbreak at my hospital too, let me through I can help."

I stared hard at the nurse, trying to look as convincing as possible. She had a quick word with someone else before nodding to let me through.

"Wear these." She said as she took me through to reception and handed me a mask, apron and latex gloves. I nodded and put them on.

"How many people are infected?" I asked, putting the mask over my face and trying to look like a real doctor.

"Ten that we know of." she replied "Two teachers and eight students."

I nodded. "Symptoms?"

"Vomiting, rashes, high temperature…" She seemed anxious. This was probably way beyond her level of training.

We went through into the main hall where they were keeping the sick; everyone else was kept in their classrooms, unable to leave until they had been tested for the virus.

I headed straight over to one of the sick teachers I recognized and sat beside her.

"Hey… Troy's mum?" She asked weakly.

I nodded, taking her hand. "Hey… Tell me what happened…"

She groaned and turned to the side as if suppressing a pain.

"It just came on so suddenly… One minute I was fine the next I was covered in a rash and vomiting…"

I felt her forehead, it was burning up and covered in beads of sweat.

"Do you know what time roughly it started?"

She nodded, "Just after lunch…"

"And you didn't leave the premises?" I asked.

She shook her head.

My phone started ringing again, it was Kayleigh. I excused myself and stepped outside to answer it.

"Hey, any update?" I asked, pulling the mask down from my face.

"The virus is airborne and causes rashes, vomiting high temperatures… That's all we know right now… Where are you, what's happening?"

"I'm in the school…" I began, leaning back on a wall and looking down the corridor towards my sons classrooms. "They've got ten sick here, I said I was a doctor and they let me in."

"Smart move, have you got the boys?"

"Not yet, they're still testing all the kids – they're not letting them leave unless they test negative. I'm going to try and convince them to let them go with me, seeing as they think I'm a doctor anyway…"

"Maybe just wait until they've done the tests…" Kayleigh interrupted, "We don't know how bad this thing could get…"

Suddenly I heard a wail, followed by a deafening scream.

"What was that?" She whispered, hearing it too.

I pulled my mask back over my mouth and headed into the main hall. The teacher I'd been sitting with was twisted in an unnatural position, her face bloated and blue, her eyes bleeding…

My hand flew up to my mouth.

"What's happening?" Kayleigh yelled.

I dropped my phone and ran over to her, turning the teacher onto her back and opening her mouth, her tongue was swollen and black, blocking her throat and choking her.

"Is she dead?" Screamed a student.

"She's choking…" I replied quickly, using my fingers to try and dislodge the swollen tongue out of her throat. It was no use… A minute later her body went limp.

"Take her into another room, don't let the kids see this…" I whispered to one of the nurses. They nodded and took her body into an office, covering it with a sheet.

"What happened?" Asked one of the kids.

I bent down and felt his forehead, he was burning up…

"She's just a bit sick…" I replied softly, squeezing his shoulder. "She'll be ok."

He nodded and went to sit back down, his face pale and sickly.

I needed to find my kids.

I started walking towards their classrooms, picking my phone up off of the floor as I left the hall. I quickly called Kayleigh back.

"Someone just died." I whispered as she answered, "Their tongue was black and swollen, they choked to death..."

Kayleigh was deathly silent.

"The same thing just happened here..." She said quietly after a few seconds.

I froze.

"What do I do?"

"Get the boys... Run." She said. I didn't need telling twice.

I put the phone in my pocket and broke into a run, turning a corner and almost breaking down the door to Troy's classroom. The kids were all reading silently at their desks and looked up startled as I entered the room.

"Troy, come on lets go." I said, waving for him to follow me.

"He hasn't been tested yet..." The teacher protested.

"It's fine I'm a doctor." I yelled, "Troy, COME ON!"

He nodded and ran to me, taking my hand and leading the way to Chase's class. It was empty.

I opened the door to the class next door, "Where have they taken Year two?" I asked, panting for breath.

The teacher looked up, surprised to see a parent and student roaming the halls freely, she hesitated before answering me.

"To the library... To be tested." She replied.

I shut the door and ran towards the library, with Troy following close behind.

The library doors were shut and locked, with a security guard standing on the other side of them. I knocked on the window and gestured for him to let us in.

"Sorry." He mouthed through the glass before turning back around, blocking my view of what they were doing to my son...

"Mum… What are they doing? Where's Chase?" Troy asked, looking up at me with his big green eyes.

"He's ok…" I replied, holding back my tears. "They're just testing him, to make sure he isn't sick…"

Troy nodded before taking a seat on the floor and leaning against my leg.

I knocked on the window again, mouthing "How long?" to the security guard.

He shrugged.

"However long it takes."

I looked at Troy, remembering the window on the other side of the library…

"Troy…" I whispered, bending down to face him.

"I'm going to go get Chase… I need you to hide somewhere and wait for me so we can get out of here safely, ok?"

He nodded, frightened.

"I'll hide over there…" He said, pointing towards a large sofa near the staff room.

I nodded, taking my mask off and putting it on him. "Perfect, I'm going to be five minutes ok, stay down, don't let anyone see you."

He tucked himself neatly behind the sofa as I ran outside into the playground, catching sight of a large puddle of bloody vomit just left of the doors.

The Library windows were all closed, I peered in and looked for my son, noticing him in a line of children, all awaiting their blood test.

I knocked softly on the window and tried to get his attention.

"Mum… What are you doing here?" He mouthed as I caught his eye.

I waved him over. "Open the window…" I whispered, gesturing for him to get the latch.

He looked around before doing as he was told.

"Where's Troy?" He said as the window creaked open.

"He's ok don't worry, just climb out, we have to get out of here…"

The other children started whispering amongst themselves as Chase climbed up onto the windowsill.

"Quickly…" I whispered, taking him under the arms and trying to lift him up and out.

The security guard noticed what was going on and started to walk over to us. "Hey!" He shouted, before stopping to cough heavily into his elbow...

"Come on!" I pulled Chase out quickly and we ran back inside to get Troy before heading back to reception.

"Get down." I whispered, noticing the small group of medical staff standing around discussing the results...

"Not one child is negative…" I overheard them say.

My heart stopped. Not one child tested negative… I looked at my boys, both looked paler than usual.

"We can't let anyone leave…" Another medic whispered.

"What will we tell the parents?"

The parents…

I gestured for the boys to stay where they were and crawled into the main office, looking for whatever button opened the gate...

"No, the gate!" I heard them yell as they ran outside to try and stop the swarm of parents now entering the school.

"Run!" I yelled, grabbing the boys and zig-zagging through the stampede.

We got out of the gate and ran down the road. There were more abandoned cars than I remember, some with people still inside. We didn't bother to get my car, there was no point – all the roads were blocked anyway, we just ran home as fast as our legs could carry us, slamming the door behind us.

"Are you ok? Come here, let me feel your heads…" I fussed, pulling both the boys close to me and checking them over for any signs of a rash or temperature… they seemed ok.

I sat them in the front room and put on cartoons while I tried to call Kayleigh.

She didn't answer. I tried to keep myself calm but I just couldn't stop imagining the worst. I was starting to feel hot and shivery, and I was sure I could see the beginnings of a rash on my hands…

"Mum…" Troy called as I tried to ring my parents. "Chase has just been sick…"

# Guy

"What's your name kid?"

Guy groaned and his eyes fluttered open. He looked around at the dark and creepy warehouse and struggled against the thick, black, leather restraints that held him fast to a cold metal chair. He wondered what they were going to do to him now that they'd caught him...

"How long was I running for?" He asked, trying to keep calm.

Leigh sat down and lit a cigarette, blowing the smoke in his face.

"About six hours." She said. "What's your name?"

He ignored her question a second time and tried to pull his hands out of the leather cuffs, but it was no use – he'd break his hands before he'd get them off. Leigh raised an eyebrow and held up two fingers, wiggling them at him until he noticed.

"What does that mean?" He asked.

She took another pull of her cigarette before answering.

"That's twice you've ignored me now." She said calmly, watching the smoke trail around her hand.

Guy nodded, remembering what his mother had said about keeping humble when they caught you...

"Sorry... It's Reece..." He said, not forgetting the other thing she said about always giving a fake name. He was lucky his mother was so clued up on these things. Other people he knew hadn't been so blessed.

"Reece, what?" Leigh smirked, happy with the way her day was going so far.

"Johnson." Guy replied. It was the only surname he could think of off the top of his head.

Leigh finished her cigarette and flicked it to the stone floor. She walked over to a desk in the corner and opened a laptop, humming to herself as she waited for it to load up.

Guy continued struggling against his restrains, trying to get a hand free as quietly as possible. It was useless. He gave up and decided to preserve his energy; surely they'd have to let him go sooner or later…

"Reece, Johnson…" Leigh mumbled as she typed the name into the system. "Let's see what we have here…"

Guy turned to face her, watching her expression change from mildly amused to downright excited.

"Well, well, well…" She giggled, turning the screen to face him.

He squinted his eyes, trying to see what she was showing him without his glasses.

"Reece Johnson, 28 years old, wanted for theft, tax evasion, unpaid student loans, insurance fraud… You're quite the little felon aren't you, Mr Johnson?" She smiled.

Guy froze. He should have guessed a name as common as Reece Johnson would carry some risk, he should have just made up a name completely…

"That's not me… You must have got the wrong man." He protested quietly, trying to look as innocent as possible.

Leigh smiled. "Oh but you see, every other Reece Johnson in this area is already registered, and since you don't have a chip – this is the only Reece Johnson you could be, unless you're lying and that's not your real name. You know it's a crime to lie to a government representative, don't you, Mr Johnson?"

Guy gulped. He could feel himself getting hot under the collar; his nerves were getting the better of him.

"I… No, I don't lie. I just… There must be other Reece Johnson's, it's a common name…"

"Not as common as you'd expect, you'd be surprised at how creative new mothers can be in this day and age. So, are you a Reece Johnson, or a liar?" She replied sternly, looking down her nose at him as though he were little more than vermin.

Guy took a deep breath and hung his head. Surely the punishment for lying would be better than the punishment for insurance fraud and tax evasion?

"My name is Guy Childs..." He muttered, defeated.

"Guy Childs..." Leigh mumbled, typing it into the system.

Just then a man walked into the room. He was tall, well over six feet and wore a dark grey suit and thick black glasses.

"So, who do we have here?" He asked, taking a seat in front of Guy.

"Guy Childs, a little liar." Leigh answered, winking at Guy as she scrolled through the page on her computer.

"A liar? No, no, no that can't be right... Surely our good community doesn't raise liars anymore?" The man replied, taking off his glasses and looking at Guy sadly.

"I know, so disappointing..." Leigh replied, shaking her head.

Guy looked around nervously, still trying to think of an escape.

"I'm sorry..." He muttered. "I wasn't thinking straight."

"No." The man replied. "You weren't."

The man walked past Guy and set his hat down on a table before taking position behind Leigh and watching the screen of her computer. His hands were behind his back and he wore an almost euphoric expression on his face as she typed away.

"He doesn't pay his council tax? What a naughty boy..."

"He hasn't voted in a few years either..." Leigh replied, tutting and shaking her head at their findings.

Guy was starting to sweat, he wasn't sure what the rules were around here but surely he couldn't be in that much trouble? It wasn't like he'd killed anyone...

"Oh my... Look at this." Leigh pointed at something on the screen, tilting it so the man could see better.

"Well, well, well." The man smiled, shaking his head and looking over to Guy. Guy began to panic.

"Anything you want to confess?" Leigh asked, leaning back in her chair and folding her arms.

Guy shook his head.

"I haven't done anything wrong…"

"Really?" The man asked, tilting his head and glared at Guy.

"You don't own a house, do you?" He asked.

Guy shook his head, confused.

"What's that got to do with anything?"

"Do you run or own a business, property, land or farm?"

"What?" Guy replied, not understanding what that had to do with anything."No."

"What do you do for work, Guy?" Leigh asked.

"I'm a… I…"

"Don't lie to us now." The man winked.

Guy sighed. "I don't have a job. I live out of motels."

"He's perfect." Leigh giggled, tapping away on her computer.

"You don't have any kids do you?" She asked.

He shook his head. "I don't really have anyone…"

The man chuckled.

"Shame." he said before turning around to face Guy.

"What's six plus eight?" He asked.

Guy thought a second before answering. "Um… fourteen?"

"Are you asking me or telling me?"

"Telling you."

The man rolled his eyes and walked away muttering "Pathetic." under his breath.

After a minute or so Leigh stood up and walked over to Guy.

"Look up." She said.

Guy looked up slowly and stared at her. She was closer to him than he thought and even though she was probably much smaller than him should he stand up, whilst tied to a chair she was rather intimidating.

"Why?" He asked.

She smiled and raised a fist.

"Because I'm about to put your lights out."

Guy froze as her clenched fist came flying towards his face, rendering him unconscious.

When he woke up again he was in what looked like an operating theatre, strapped down to a table with more thick leather restraints.

"Hello?" He called out, hoping he had been found and taken to a nearby hospital. There was no answer.

He called again but still no answer came. He decided to wait...

A few hours went by before anyone came, but just as he thought he was about to fall asleep – a woman entered. A woman he didn't recognize.

"Hello." She smiled.

Guy looked up and cleared his throat. "Hello..." He replied nervously. "Where am I?"

The woman flounced into the room and stood at his bedside smiling. "You are in one of the best facilities in North Carolina, so don't you worry, we're going to have you fixed up in no time."

Guy frowned, not knowing what she meant by 'fixed up'. Had he broken something?

"My name is Valarie..." She continued. "I'll be your head programmer so any details you want to fine-tune you just let me know and I'll get it sorted. Questions?"

Guy stared hard in confusion.

"Yes." he said, not knowing quite where to start. "What's going on?"

Valarie laughed.

"Possession, dear Guy. We're calling you up for duty."

Guy was more confused than ever.

"What duty?" He asked, pulling against his restraints.

Valarie sighed and sat on the edge of his bed.

"Didn't you get a briefing earlier when they brought you in?"

He shook his head.

"No, I got punched in the face."

Valarie giggled.

"Sorry about that, they can be a little rough…"

Guy frowned, not knowing what the hell this woman was on about. She sounded crazy. Was she even a real nurse?

"What do you mean I'm being called for duty? What's possession? Please just tell me what's going on…" He pleaded with her, on the edge of desperation and verging on insanity.

Valarie stroked his face lovingly.

"We're going to re-program you. We're going to make you useful again." She smiled, picking up a file that was tucked into a metal box at the end of his bed.

"What do you mean? What's that?" Guy asked, trembling with a fearful confusion.

"This is your file. At the moment your avatar is being wasted. You have no job, no home, no prospects and no value. We're going to fix that, we're going to make you a productive member of society with just a small procedure…"

Guy flinched as Valarie reached out towards him. She giggled and wiped the beads of sweat from his forehead.

"Why do you look so worried?" She asked. "There's no need to be… It happens to everyone eventually… You won't remember a thing."


A few days later Guy woke up. He was in a new room, in a new bed – this time without restraints. He awoke softly to the sound of violins. As he sat up and looked around a nurse entered the room.

"Good morning Sir." She smiled, placing a tray on the table next to his bed. "How are you feeling?"

"Confused…" Guy replied. "Where am I?"

"You're in hospital." She replied. "You were in a pretty nasty accident. But don't worry, you're all fixed now and ready to get back to work."

Guy nodded, reaching out for the glass of water on the tray the nurse had placed next to him.

"And… Who am I exactly?" He asked.

The nurse smiled. "Why, you're Senator Harry Child's… Remember? Now eat up, your car will be here soon."

"Right, yes of course…" Child's hastily replied as the memories of law school and local elections began to form.

# The Children of Wolfpit

I'm sure you've heard all about the green children of Wolfpit.

No?

Alright then, I'll tell you...

It happened in the 12th Century, sometime during the reign of King Stephan. It's called Wolfpit because of the huge wolf pits the farmers would dig. You see, there were a lot of wolves around in those times and farmers wanted to protect their livestock, so around their farms they began to dig these holes the wolves would fall into should they wander too close.

One morning, a farmer went out to check the pits for any wolves that had fallen in during the night. It was quite something to catch a wolf; their skins were used for clothing and rugs while their meat was saved for only the finest of dining. The people at the time believed deeply that you become what you put in your body, consuming a wolf would only bring strength and bravery.

As the farmer got closer to the pit he could hear something shuffling about and grew excited at the thought of catching such a sought after creature. He was a poor man, and wolf meat sold for quite a bit back then. Looking into the deep, dark hole the farmer realized it wasn't a wolf that had fallen into his pit, but rather two small children.

The children, he noticed, had almost glowing green skin and wore clothing made from unknown materials.

"Margery, come quick!" He called to his wife who promptly came rushing over.

"What is it?" She asked as she reached his side, gasping in amazement as the farmer directed her gaze to the children in the pit.

"Heaven's!" She cried. "Fetch a ladder, quick!"

It wasn't long before the farmer had retrieved the poor, shivering children and taken them back to his house where they awaited the village doctor.

Neither of the children spoke a word of English, nor did they eat any of the food offered to them by the farmer and his wife, instead they fed upon raw peas and drank only the smallest sips of warm water.

Well, the doctor had never seen anything like it and hastily sent for a second opinion, then a third and a fourth…

No one could explain the children's green skin, nor did they recognize the language they spoke. It was all very strange, even down to their mannerisms and the way they interacted with each other – almost animalistic. After a while the farmer and his wife decided to keep and raise the two children as their own.

Over time the children adapted their diets and began to learn English. The farmer's wife even gave them name's and birthdays – as a devout Christian; she called the girl Mary and the boy Joseph.

Around a year or so after the children had been found, the boy grew sick. He took to his bed, growing weaker and weaker by the day. No one could figure out what was wrong with him and many a doctor came and went, prescribing new medicines that proved unsuccessful for the strange boy.

As the boy grew closer and closer to death, his adoptive mother's search for a miracle cure became frantic. She travelled far and wide, looking for anyone that would try to help poor Joseph. Eventually, she came across a coven of Witches from Suffolk who agreed to help the child. With no one else to turn to, Margery accepted their help. The coven travelled back with her to the farm and formed a circle around the boy.

The farmer, his wife and little Mary sat in another room – waiting desperately for some good news. After what felt like an eternity, the high priestess of the witches emerged from the boys' room and asked to speak with Mary.

"Her English isn't very good…" The farmer's wife began, aware the little girl wouldn't be much help with the language barrier.

The witch smiled and took the girl outside, sitting with her on the grass.

"Dem harishenra que to do?" The witch spoke.

Mary looked up, recognizing the language instantly.

"Do enra to aquister undo enmei..." She replied.

The farmer and his wife stood at the door, listening on in shock. No one had been able to communicate with the children in their native language before. What was it? Finnish? German? Spanish? They had no idea...

"Kraan de andu, el ri ha ku do." The witch responded softly, stroking the little girl's hair and placing a small yellow flower behind her ear. Mary looked up at the witch and smiled, a smile rarely seen by the folk of Wolfpit.

"De ri un to a dien." The child whispered back.

The exchange went on for a few minutes and to this day no one quite knows what was said, but when they re-entered the house – suddenly Mary could both speak and understand English perfectly.

"What... I don't understand..." Muttered Margery upon hearing Mary speak English for the first time.

The witch smiled.

"These children are very special..." She began, waiting for Mary to disappear into her brother's room before she spoke more in depth about the children and what she had discovered.

"What do you mean special?" The farmer asked.

"They are quite unlike any other human you know of. A rare and dying breed, if you will..."

"Of what?" Margery asked nervously.

The witch smiled. "In our language we call them 'Lycosias', but to you, I guess you would call them the wolf people."

Margery froze, not quite knowing how to reply. The farmer laughed.

"You've got to be joking." He chuckled. "Werewolves don't exist – what absolute rubbish."

The witches smile faded into a frown accompanied by a low growl.

"You should be more careful about what you tarnish as folklore, human. To members of the sea, you are but a fairytale."

The farmer closed his mouth and inhaled loudly, displeased about being spoken down to by a woman – but he said nothing about it.

"The children fell into your pit whilst they were in their natural form. Their skin is green because a wolf's diet is not suited to promote a healthy complexion in humans. The language they speak is the tongue of the Lycosias – only their kind and a handful of witches can understand and speak it."

The farmer rolled his eyes, still not ready to believe the witches words.

"What about the boy... Can you help him?" Margery asked desperately.

The witch smiled sadly.

"We can take him back with us. We cannot heal him, but we can help him to pass in peace."

Margery wailed, heartbroken that the boy she had taken in as her own couldn't be saved. The witch took her hand reassuringly, kissing her palm.

"Why do you cry?" She asked.

Margery wiped her tears and choked back her sobs as she tried to form her words.

"I just... I'm not ready to lose him." She sniffed. "He's my son..."

The witch nodded.

"You cry for selfish reasons." She replied bluntly. "The boy will find peace in death – be happy for him. Glad that he is finally able to rest without pain."

Margery nodded, not wanting to offend the witch. "I'm sorry..." She whispered.

"Don't be." The witch replied. "You are only human."

A little while later the witches had made a sling, which they hung at the side of a large horse for the boy to sit in while they travelled.

"The girl wishes to stay with you." The witch said to Margery before they left. "I trust you will raise her well?"

Margery nodded. "She will want for nothing…"

"Very well." responded the witch, looking down at Mary and stroking her fine hair.

"Diem a to unauris da rona… Dis emartu, be na." She said softly.

The little girl nodded and kissed the palm of the witch's hand.

"Um to en darato…"

Over the years Mary adopted the diet of the villagers completely, allowing her skin to turn to a normal complexion. Margery enrolled her into a good school and raised her well, just as she promised the witch she would. At age 27 Mary married a wealthy man and moved away from the farm, going on to have her own children and naming her first born son after her dear brother Joseph.

By the time she was in her mid-30's Mary fell gravely ill. Her husband sought the best doctors he could find but no one could recommend a cure or work out what was causing her illness. Mary, although she never said – knew exactly what was wrong. As time went by Mary grew weaker and weaker, until she could no longer stand without aid.

One day, as Mary grew closer to death – a knock came at the door.

"Tu a diem do sia no…" A soft voice whispered in her ear.

Mary's eyes fluttered open and looked up. There before her, stood the same witch from all those years ago, she hadn't aged a day.

"Do a natues…" Mary replied, smiling up at the witch.

The witch sat down beside her and stroked her fine hair, tucking a yellow flower behind her ear.

"Are you ready, little one?" The witch asked.

Mary nodded, and with the help of the witch stood on her feet and walked slowly towards the door.

"We cannot cure her, but we can help her pass without pain…"

Mary breathed a heavy sigh, hearing the witch tell her husband the same thing she had told her mother all those years ago. Her husband kissed Mary on the cheek one final time and bid her farewell, his eyes glistening with tears as he watched his beloved leave in a sling on the side of a horse.

When Mary awoke, she found herself lying on a bed of soft grass and flowers. She didn't feel any pain, and no longer was her body weak and fragile. She sat herself up and looked around; noticing how quiet it was as the winds gently blew the grass around her paws.

"Welcome home…" Someone growled from behind her. She turned around quickly, surprised at the unexpected voice.

Behind her sat a large, grey wolf. Mary frowned, studying his soft brown eyes that looked strangely familiar…

She smiled, realizing who it was that sat so majestically before her.

He hadn't changed a bit.

Well, apart from the fur.

They say that Mary's children all carried the wolf gene and passed it down to her descendants. To this day, hundreds of werewolves still live among us, most of them have adapted so well into human life that they don't even know what they are…

# The Worlds Below

"Oh bugger it." came the frustrated groans of an old woman as a set of keys dropped to the floor, waking the sleeping boy.

"Shh." Someone else whispered.

The boy, whose name changed depending on what realm he was waking up in, awoke with a start. He sat up and turned to face the odd pair.

"Don't say anything." The old man whispered, raising a finger to his lips. He pointed to a notepad and pencil that sat on a bedside table to the boys left.

"Write it all down."

The boy nodded and began writing down the strange events of his dream. It wasn't long before it all came flooding back to him; the striking distant world stuck out like a sore thumb. So full of life and colour, not at all like the others.

"I've tried that one." The woman huffed, placing her balled up fists onto her rounded hips in a display of her annoyance. They'd been through almost a hundred keys already and not one had fit the lock on the small wooden door of the cold, stone, empty room. The boy finished writing and set the notepad down by his side, fingering the pages as he thought quietly to himself.

"None of the keys fit..." He mumbled after a few moments.

The old man stopped fumbling with the keys immediately and turned around with the old woman to face the boy.

"We know." He said, a look of confusion on his face.

The boy frowned.

"So why are you still trying to open it?"

The old man and woman looked at each other as if the boy had completely lost his mind.

"What else would you suggest we do?" The old man asked.

The boy thought for a moment before answering.

"Just stop."

It was an odd suggestion. So simple, yet so foreign. Neither one of them had ever thought to 'just stop' before.

"But this is what we do..." the old woman began, her voice trailing off as she looked over to the old man.

"This is all we've ever done." He added, shrugging his shoulders. Neither one of them could comprehend doing anything else.

The boy frowned.

"How long have we been here?" He asked, his brain still fuzzy from his sleep.

"We've always been here." Said the old lady. "Ever since we can remember."

The boy stood up and walked over to the door. He stared at it for a moment before cocking his head to the side, his mind whirring through all the memories he had of this old wooden door, with its brass hinges. He couldn't remember a time he'd ever tried to open it before, which could only mean he hadn't.

The old man and woman stared open mouthed as the young boy reached out towards the door. He rested his hand on the handle for a moment before turning it and opening the door slowly. The door was heavy, it creaked and groaned as it opened – but it opened nonetheless.

"It was never locked..." the old man whispered.

"Never locked." The old woman repeated.

The boy said nothing. He stared forward at the world outside of the small room they'd been stuck in for all of eternity. It wasn't much, just a corridor with other doors identical to the one he'd just opened, but it was more than he'd ever known before.

"Look at this!" The old woman cried as she ran forwards and out of the door, her head swinging from left to right as she looked the place up and down.

"This is fantastic!"

The old man stepped through the door curiously, the movements of his head copying those of the old woman's as his gaze travelled the length of the corridor.

"How bizarre."

The young boy smiled; an expression he rarely wore. He hadn't expected the door to open so easily. He took a step forward and crossed the threshold into the corridor.

Suddenly, the whole world began to vibrate. It was soft at first, almost unnoticeable, but within a matter of milliseconds it was rumbling as though a volcano were about to erupt right through the floor.

"Get back in the room!" Yelled the old man.

The young boy froze in fear as the old woman and the old man came pelting past him at speeds mostly unreachable by folk of their age.

"Come on!"

The old man grabbed the young boy by his arm and pulled him back into the room, slamming the door shut behind him.

"What are we thinking?!" He cried.

"Quick, everyone, back into places!"

The trio scrambled about the room, picking up keys and getting back into the bed. As soon as they were back in their normal positions, the rumbling stopped.

"I don't get it..." the boy frowned, his confusion etching temporary wrinkles into his young face.

"We're not supposed to." Muttered the old man as he handed the keys to the old woman, who promptly picked one at random and stuck it into the lock, giving it a jiggle.

"What do you mean?" The young boy whispered.

"Don't you want to leave? Don't you want to know what's out there?"

"Not this one..." the old woman murmured softly, as though in a trance.

"That's not our business. This is what we do. This is our moment in time. There're other versions of ourselves out there that get to leave the room, not us."

"But why?" The boy asked.

The old lady sighed.

"It's how the world stays balanced. We all have our place, our purpose, and we do it forever. It's just how things are." She chose another key sadly. "Go back to sleep. You're lucky you can sleep – at least you get to leave in your dreams."

The boy lay down and tried to close his eyes, but the jingling of keys and mutters of "oh bugger it" from the old woman kept him awake.

He wondered what the other versions of him did once they left the room. What had they seen? Who had they become?

He rolled onto his side and looked over at the old man.

"Do I have a name?" He asked.

The old man shrugged.

"I haven't the foggiest."

# Abduction

It was a Thursday. I remember because that's the day he used to play football after school. We'd gone for a pizza afterwards, which was just what we did on Thursdays – it was our little father/son tradition.

We left the pizza place later than usual. It was pretty busy that night due to some gig that was happening at Wembley stadium, so there was a bit of a wait for a table. I don't think we started heading back until nearly 7.

"Are you and Evelyn going to get married?" He asked. I remember the look on his face, he didn't want me to – he was nervous of my new partner. Ever since his mother passed, change had been difficult for him and he wasn't used to her just yet. It was early days still.

"No kiddo, we're not getting married, don't you worry." I replied, smiling weakly. I wasn't quite sure what he wanted to hear but I hoped that was it. I wasn't looking to re-marry anytime soon and Evelyn had kids of her own – we were taking things slow.

We talked about his guitar lessons a bit. He wasn't happy with his teacher and he was having trouble placing his fingers on the right strings, it was all getting a bit overwhelming for him. I tried to talk to him about football – something he and I both enjoyed – eventually getting a smile out of him. It was just after that it happened. We had just passed Brent Cross on the A41 when I realized the roads were suddenly completely clear of any other cars. There were no people to be seen, no lights on in the buildings, no planes in the sky, even the radio had gone silent. I slowed down momentarily; taking in the strange scene before speeding up again, wanting to get away as fast as I could.

It took a long time for me to remember much of this – but after years of hypnotherapy I've started to recall even the smallest of details. Like the way I looked at him, his little face staring up at me – wondering what was going on and if he should be afraid, or the way my eyes watered and my body shuddered as a bright, burning white light engulfed us both...

As soon as it had come, it had gone, and we were driving down the A41 again, only now we were at Apex Corner and it was an hour and a half later. My phone was dead and there were cars around us again. Neither of us could really speak for a minute or so, we were dazed, but certain that something strange had just taken place. We weren't sure exactly what, we had no memory other than the empty road and a light and even that was foggy, like a dream – but we just knew. As I pulled up onto the drive Denny grabbed at my jacket and began to sob.

"What happened Dad?" He whispered, tugging my arm towards him. "What was that?"

The truth is I had absolutely no idea. I was terrified myself, I didn't know if we'd died and were now ghosts, if we'd suffered seizures or been transported to another dimension for 90 minutes... My head was pounding, like I was coming down off of something. I wanted to sob alongside him.

I picked him up and pulled him onto my lap. He was shaking with fear and buried his face deep into the grey fleece I was wearing under my jacket, not caring about the awkward way his legs were hanging over the handbrake. I carried him inside and lay with him on his bed as he cried and shouted angrily about what had just happened to him – he could remember far more than I and after listening to his story I not only understood his tears – I was crying them for him. I could feel myself getting angry. I rang an old friend of mine; Angela, a police officer from Kingsbury. Within fifteen minutes I had police officers and a medic in my house, sitting around the dining room table with myself and Denny, discussing the peculiar events of that evening.

Denny was no longer crying, instead he was just confused and exhausted – as was I.

"We were in a white room. There were six of them, and they were doing things to us with long silver sticks. We couldn't move..." He said as the officers took notes.

I'd listened to his story around twenty times by now and I was started to get images in my mind of what had happened to us. I think the white light that I had seen after all the cars disappeared was actually the white light in the room, but because I had some kind of 'time distorting type filter' over my memories where, well, I guess they must have drugged us or something – my brain had turned the white light of the room into a quick, blinding flash. I tried hard to remember more and make sense of things, I could picture what Denny was saying but were they my memories or was I just putting images to his words? I wasn't sure. I told Angela what I was thinking nonetheless.

"I have no other explanation for it and I know it sounds crazy, but I think something took us. Something took us and did some kind of medical experiments on us, and they tried to wipe our memories of it after."

Angela had stopped taking my statement and we were outside having a cigarette at this point. We'd known each other since primary school and had been friends for over thirty years; I knew I could talk to her. I knew she'd help.

"Do you remember if they spoke to you?" She asked. "Denny said they spoke to him in his head, do you remember any kind of psychic communication?"

Her attention to detail and professionalism had always impressed me, I felt immensely reassured to have her on my side with this, but I had to shake my head sadly. I couldn't remember a thing.

Denny told us the 'tall men' had said they were coming back for him, he was pretty scared – as you can imagine a seven year old would be. Stefan, (Angela's partner) said he'd keep watch on us for the next few weeks just to be sure, and panic alarms were set up around the house. Angela recommended (off record) a shot of whiskey and a long sleep, which I thoroughly agreed to. They left around 2am, by that time Denny was fast asleep on the sofa.

I thought about carrying him upstairs and putting him to bed, but I was so worried about waking him that I left him to sleep on the sofa that night. I sat in the armchair on the other side of the room, watching him sleep and making sure he was ok.

He didn't go to school the next day, I kept him off and let him watch Disney films and play with his toys – which helped a lot, so did ice cream. I just wanted to keep an eye on him…

Angela called and said they'd found skid marks, some near Brent Cross and more at Apex corner, she said they were made by the same tires – which of course matched my car. There were no marks in between. She also said that every CCTV camera in the area for some reason went dark around the time I said I saw all the cars disappear. Things just seemed to get weirder.

It got to about 4pm before Denny and I spoke about the events of the previous evening. We were both still pretty shaken up. I called Evelyn and asked if we could stay at hers that night, I thought it might be good for Denny to be around other people. I think it was. The boys played in the garden for most of the evening before watching films in the front room whilst I updated Evelyn on our strange situation.

"Why didn't you call me?" She asked, handing me a rum and coke – her 'go to' drink.

I shrugged. "I didn't want to worry you." Truth was if I did call her she'd have come straight over and I didn't think that would have been right on Denny whilst everything was still so fresh.

"We had the police round, there was a lot happening." I replied sadly, having still not quite processed the situation myself. We talked for a while about it all before heading to bed.

That was the night we had the first nightmares, Denny and I. We both dreamt we were back in that white room. I saw myself having my left eyeball removed and something being inserted into the socket, Denny saw himself being sliced open from his lower abdomen to his chest. We were both pretty shaken up to say the least.

Evelyn called me every day after that. I welcomed those calls. I'd never felt so lost.

The next Monday Denny and I started therapy. Neither of us were great at opening up about our feelings anyway – but this was just crazy, it was unreal, bizarre. We couldn't process it, let alone explain it again – we'd already done that twenty times over to the police and still couldn't make sense of it. It didn't help that the first thing the therapist said to us was; "So you believe you were abducted by aliens? Tell me about that…" We found a new therapist shortly after.

Six weeks later Denny had started getting back to normal. He was playing and smiling more, being cheeky again and the colour in his cheeks returned. For a while he just looked pale and haunted, like he was suffering from a terrible illness – it was fear. He wasn't scared anymore; he'd seemingly dealt with it and moved on. I was happy for him and didn't mention it at all after that, but I still couldn't process it myself. It made me sick to think about, the fact someone had taken my boy, done things to him, hurt him, scared him and I wasn't able to do anything about it. It was my worst fear come to life.

A month later was Christmas. I'd taken him into central London to see the lights. We'd gone to winter wonderland and done some last minute Christmas shopping. We'd had dinner at My Old Dutch, a pancake house and sung Christmas songs on the train home. We got off the train at Queensbury and picked up my car from my office car park. I don't really remember what we talked about… It all happened so fast.

One minute we were just sitting there talking, driving home… The next, it was like we were flashing, fading in and out of reality. I could see the white room again, the light. I could see Denny's panicked face, his tear filled eyes as they stared hard into mine. It was happening again.

Three hours later I woke up in a side road near Canons Park. My car was about 100 yards away from me and I was lying face down in the middle of the road. I came round to a woman screaming at me, thinking I'd been hit by my own car and was the victim of a terrible accident. She ran over and helped me to my feet as I stumbled around, dazed and confused.

"Where's Denny?" I asked, noticing the empty passenger seat of my car.

The woman looked at me, not knowing who or what I was on about – she hadn't seen anyone but me.

I knew exactly what had happened. I could feel it in the pit of my stomach. Like the Earth had fallen away from under me and I was sinking into nothingness.

"Where's Denny?" I asked again, choking on my own voice. I couldn't stop saying it.

"Where's my boy… Where's my son…"

An ambulance was called and I managed to dial Angela's number and thrust my phone into the woman's hands, telling her to give her my location and to tell her "They took him." The woman did as she was told and within what felt like a matter of seconds police cars and a forensic team had appeared.

Angela rushed to my side, catching me as I fell into her arms. I couldn't breathe.

"They took him… They came back… They took him…" Was all I could say, I was in shock.

She took me to the hospital and I was checked over. They found high levels of an unknown substance in my blood, so I was given an MRI. It was then we discovered something had been implanted in me, a small disk shape object, made of flexible, metallic material. It was behind my left eyeball.

It's been 2 years since they took Denny. I don't know why they took him, I don't know why they want him, or what they're doing to him. I just want him home.

Please, if you're reading this… Whoever you are…

Please bring my boy home.

# An Interview with the Devil

I don't really know when the first time I saw him was. It's like he's always been there, a shadow in the corner of the room or a breath on the back of my neck. He felt like a man, old and powerful, I can't explain how but I just had these feelings, it wasn't like he was one man – he could change into something different at will. He just mostly appeared as a man to me. Maybe he was trying to intimidate me or something. If he was it worked. I used to run from my bedroom to the bathroom when he appeared, slamming the door shut and locking it once I was safely inside. I could feel him on the stairs, watching me. The first time I ever felt him touch me I was around 10, he tapped my head with his cold, bony finger to wake me up; hard. When I was 12 he squeezed my hand and whispered my name loudly while I was lining up with my class at school. I spun around to see who it was but no one was that close to me. I knew it was him. I grew paranoid, fearful and depressed. I felt haunted, tormented, burdened. People sensed that, boys at school would call me damaged goods, girls would call me a freak. The phrase 'You're different' became a part of my everyday experience, like people could tell there was something dark going on in my life they just couldn't put their finger on it, and nobody thought to ask.

He could make things happen, his power was limitless. He could even possess and manipulate the people close to me without them realizing. He would tell me what my future held, in the darkest hour of night whilst the rest of the house where soundly sleeping. He would play out images of the darkest parts of my future in my head just before I slept. He'd tell me how I'd move out before I was ready, I'd be vulnerable and targeted. All this information about the worst and most difficult parts of my life he'd pump into my head from as early as I could remember, never the good things. I spent my life in fear, waiting to be attacked. I felt helpless. Everything happened just as he said it would.

The day after my child had been conceived he told me I was pregnant on the bus. I was on my way to college. I caught my reflection in the window and as soon as I did it was like someone next to me said out loud; "You're pregnant." I just stared at myself, knowing it was true. He stayed with me through the pregnancy, giving me dreams of my future child with a red mark on her forehead, a sign of him. I told him what I wanted her to look like, what date I wanted her to be born, I said if he was real to make it happen – he did, every word of it.

After that he changed, rarely trying to scare or intimidate me but more often offering guidance and companionship. Sometimes he went back to his old ways, drifting through temporary phases of causing me distress and suffering, but he'd go back to his gentle new self after a little while.

About a year ago he left me. No words, no explanation, he just left. One night he was there, watching me from the hallway, the next I couldn't feel him. I didn't feel him again until recently. My brother had stayed round my house and I woke up to someone tapping my head, hard – just like he did back then. Immediately I rolled over, hoping to find my brother smiling at me and suggesting breakfast. He was fast asleep and facing the other way.

Since then I feel him everywhere, stronger than ever, and today was the biggest encounter we'd had as of yet.

Right now I'm sitting on my bed, a while ago I was on the floor in my front room. The noise in my head from him talking at me had become overwhelming. I sat down, at first to gather myself and breathe, and then to respond. I took some sage out from the kitchen cupboard and took it upstairs to my bedroom. I lit it, turning slowly and creating a smoke circle around myself before sitting on the bed and opening up my laptop, I decided I would capture our first real conversation.

I felt my eyes welling up with tears as I thought of what to say, what would my first question be? I closed my eyes and thought for a moment, taking some deep breaths and relaxing into the silence.

Him: "You're over thinking this."

Me: "Where did you go?"

Him: "I was sleeping."

Me: "Why are you back?"

Him: "I am awake."

Me: "Why me?"

Him: "Why anyone?"

Me: "Don't do that, just talk to me. I don't understand."

Him: "What would you like to understand?"


I feel a weight on the bed, like he just sat down in front of me. I feel like he's smiling.


Me: "Who are you?"

Him: "Everything you are, and everything you're not. We are products of the same thing, you and I."

Me: "Explain."

Him: "You already know."

Me: "I want to hear you say it."

Him: "You don't believe this is real?"

Me: "More than anything, but I need to hear you say it."

Him: "There is beauty in not knowing, you know?"

Me: "How would you know, you know everything?"

Him: "Not yet. That is why I still exist."

Me: "What are you?"

Him: "I am everything."

Me: "Am I everything too?"

Him: "Yes. Right now you are just having an experience with a body."

Me: "You don't have one?"

Him: "Not like yours."

Me: "What are you?"

Him: "A ghost maybe. I don't have a name for myself, but you have many."

Me: "A demon?"

Him: "Perhaps."

Me: "Where you human once?"

Him: "Many times."

Me: "What about me?"

Him: "You have been like me before too, everyone has."

Me: "Are you good or bad?"

Him: "There is no good or bad, only subjectivity."

Me: "You tortured me, my whole life."

Him: "I was teaching you."

Me: "Teaching me what?"

Him: "To find peace, you must first study anarchy."

Me: "So… You caused me pain to give me peace?"

Him: "To find control, you must know how it feels to be helpless."

Me: "I was a child."

Him: "No, your human shell was just young."

# Woman in White

I'm still groggy from my sleep but I can make out her shape in the darkness. She's tall, much taller than me and her hair drapes over her shoulders as she sways gently from side to side. She stands hunched by my window in a quiet sadness. I think I awoke because her whimpering disturbed me. I have a vague memory of her cries seeping back into my brain...

"Are you ok?" I ask. I don't know why. I should have yelled at her to get out, or at the very least asked how she found her way in. She doesn't respond. She barely moves.

"Who are you?" I ask, my voice a little louder this time just in case she didn't hear me. She still doesn't answer me, but she lifts her head a little, just enough for me to catch a glimpse of her dark eyes.

"I thought you were sleeping..." She whispers.

I reach out for her, I don't know why, it just felt natural to do so. She comes and sits by me, her hand resting on mine while her other strokes my hair.

"I've missed you." She whispers in the dark.

I don't know why she says that, or even who she is, but I smile and allow her to continue.

"After I buried you, I never thought I'd see you again..."

That's when it all comes back.

The fire, the burning, the pain. I died before. Yet here I am again, experiencing a new life, in a world that has changed so much since I last saw it.

"Honey..." I whisper.

"I'm not dead anymore... You are."

From the Author:

A special thanks to all who have read my book and made it this far, it has been my absolute pleasure to write this for all you weird kids out there and I hope you'll consider picking up any other books I release in the future.

Blessed be, and to all a good life.

To Emily, Timothy, Bethany and Leena;

The Vampire, The Dragon, The Mermaid and The Witch,

Thank you for keeping me sane.

Printed in Great Britain
by Amazon

43491252R00109